"If you've no obj... company..."

Simon had always been considerate that way, Annabel remembered with a bittersweet pang. At least, until the tragedy of Lily's death had changed him, turning him into a closed, distant stranger.

"Let's just play it by ear," she said, keeping her tone light. "Is your hotel far from here?"

The firm, well-shaped lips she'd always found so irresistible—and still did, she realized with a tremor—eased into the familiar curved smile she'd thought lost forever, at least to her. Seeing it again gave her spirits a lift. "Actually, I'm staying here," he said. "Fourth floor."

She almost missed her step. Staying here? On the floor above hers? Maybe his room, his bed, were directly over hers. How would she ever be able to sleep, knowing he was so close to her, just a few floorboards separating them?

Dear Reader,

Well, as promised, the dog days of summer have set in, which means one last chance at the beach reading that's an integral part of this season (even if you do most of it on the subway, like I do!). We begin with *The Beauty Queen's Makeover* by Teresa Southwick, next up in our MOST LIKELY TO… miniseries. She was the girl "most likely to" way back when, and he was the awkward geek. Now they've all but switched places, and the fireworks are about to begin….

In *From Here to Texas*, Stella Bagwell's next MEN OF THE WEST book, a Navajo man and the girl who walked out on him years ago have to decide if they believe in second chances. And speaking of second chances (or first ones, anyway), picture this: a teenaged girl obsessed with a gorgeous college boy writes down some of her impure thoughts in her diary, and buries said diary in the walls of an old house in town. Flash forward ten-ish years, and the boy, now a man, is back in town—and about to dismantle the old house, brick by brick. Can she find her diary before he does? Find out in Christine Flynn's finale to her GOING HOME miniseries, *Confessions of a Small-Town Girl*. In *Everything She's Ever Wanted* by Mary J. Forbes, a traumatized woman is finally convinced to come out of hiding, thanks to the one man she can trust. In Nicole Foster's *Sawyer's Special Delivery*, a man who's played knight-in-shining armor gets to do it again—to a woman (cum newborn baby) desperate for his help, even if she hates to admit it. And in *The Last Time I Saw Venice* by Vivienne Wallington, a couple traumatized by the loss of their child hopes that the beautiful city that brought them together can work its magic—one more time.

So have your fun. And next month it's time to get serious—about reading, that is….

Enjoy!

Gail Chasan
Senior Editor

Please address questions and book requests to:
Silhouette Reader Service
U.S.: 3010 Walden Ave., P.O. Box 1325, Buffalo, NY 14269
Canadian: P.O. Box 609, Fort Erie, Ont. L2A 5X3

The Last Time I Saw Venice

VIVIENNE WALLINGTON

Silhouette®

SPECIAL EDITION®

Published by Silhouette Books

America's Publisher of Contemporary Romance

SILHOUETTE BOOKS

ISBN 0-373-24704-4

THE LAST TIME I SAW VENICE

Copyright © 2005 by Vivienne Wallington

Books by Vivienne Wallington

Silhouette Special Edition

In Her Husband's Image #1608
The Last Time I Saw Venice #1704

Silhouette Romance

Claiming his Bride #1515
Kindergarten Cupids #1596

Previously published under the pseudonym Elizabeth Duke

Harlequin Romance/Mills & Boon

Softly Flits a Shadow #2425
Windarra Stud #2871
Wild Temptation #3068
Island Deception #3095
Fair Trial #3366
Whispering Vines #3656
Outback Legacy #H3817
Bogus Bride #H3911
Shattered Wedding #H4071
Make-Believe Family #H4279
To Catch a Playboy #H4297
Heartless Stranger #H4392
Takeover Engagement #H4585

Taming a Husband #H4663
The Marriage Pact #H4727
Look-Alike Fiancée #H4874
The Husband Dilemma #H4950
The Parent Test #H5111
Outback Affair #H5158

VIVIENNE WALLINGTON

lives in Melbourne, Australia. Previously a librarian and children's writer, she now writes romance full-time. Reading, family and travel are her other main interests. She has written nineteen Harlequin Romance novels under the pseudonym Elizabeth Duke and now writes for Silhouette Books under her real name. Vivienne and her husband, John, have a daughter and son and five wonderful grandchildren. She would love to hear from readers, who can write to her c/o Silhouette Books, 233 Broadway, Suite 1001, New York, NY 10279 or e-mail viv.wallington@bigpond.com.

To Karin, who loves Venice, too.

Chapter One

Annabel gazed across the sparkling Venetian Lagoon and couldn't believe she was here, that she'd actually come back.

Romantic Venice...city of dreams and fantasies.

Crushed dreams, fizzled fantasies.

No! Her chin came up. She'd thrashed all this out in her mind before leaving chilly, wet London, and decided it was worth risking a few bittersweet memories. Venice was where she'd been happy once, where she and Simon had met and shared the most rapturous few days—and unforgettable nights—of their lives. All her memories of Venice were joyful ones. It was the trauma and heartbreak that had followed later in Sydney that she didn't want to dwell on.

And she wouldn't! She was here to relax, to recuperate from the flu and pneumonia, and to luxuriate in the soothing magic of Venice.

Everything was just as she remembered, just as magical…the quaint canals and arched bridges, the ever-changing light, the graceful Gothic palaces and grand churches, the buzzing water traffic—and the same hordes of swarming tourists.

And this time she was one of them. Four years ago, she'd been here for a law conference, to learn more about her chosen career. To an ambitious, hardworking Sydney lawyer who'd never been to Europe, it was a dream come true when her firm had sent her to Venice for a week.

A dream in more ways than one, she thought, her eyes misting. On her very first day in Venice, another more heart-stopping dream had materialized.

Painful as it was to think of Simon, her memories of their first meeting and their blossoming romance in Venice were still sweet, still as filled with a piquant nostalgia as a dim, happy dream. The unbelievable *way* they'd met still brought a smile to her lips, even now.

She let her gaze veer back across the water, seeking out the glossy black gondolas moving with leisurely skill between the other faster boats.

Four years ago, she'd taken a gondola ride along the Grand Canal with a group of fellow conference delegates. If she hadn't stupidly decided to stand up on the seat to take some photographs, she might never have met Simon. A water taxi had swished past at the vital moment, creating a wave that made the gondola rock precariously. She'd lost her balance and tumbled overboard, landing with a splash and a gasp of shock in the cold, deep green water of the Grand Canal.

It was Simon, the sole passenger in the water taxi, who had dived in to save her as she surfaced, his boat having immediately circled and come back. With a strong arm clamped round her waist, he'd dragged her to his hovering water taxi. Her friends in the gondola had cheered and waved before continuing on their way, confident they were leaving her in good hands.

She smiled, remembering her first proper look at her husky, dark-haired rescuer as he'd helped her into a seat. He had the physique of an Olympic athlete and the bluest eyes she'd ever seen; he looked incredibly sexy, with his black hair still dripping and sunlit rivulets running down his strong, chiseled face.

She recalled how she'd blinked up at him as he'd checked her over, mesmerized by the beads of water sparkling on the ends of his dark eyelashes, above the brilliant sheen of his eyes. Water was streaming from her own hair and rolling down her face and shirt, making her acutely conscious that her soaked T-shirt, with only a flimsy sports bra beneath, did nothing to hide the nub of her nipples or the rounded curve of her breasts.

She'd thought him Italian at first sight, a classic Romeo with that black hair and those piercing blue eyes. But the moment he spoke, she realized he was Australian, just like herself. An Australian with an Italian name—Pacino—and an Italian grandfather. He was working in New York at the time, training with one of the world's top neurosurgeons. He'd come to Italy to give a medical lecture at Padua University and was only in Venice for four days before heading back to New York, while she had to go back to Sydney at the end of the week.

But they'd had four days, and she'd willingly skipped the odd lecture or two for the chance to see more of him…

"Annabel?"

A woman's voice—as Australian as her own—intruded on her pleasantly poignant memories. For a moment, she failed to respond, her mind still far away. Four long years away.

"Annabel…it *is* you, isn't it?" A hand touched her arm, a very real hand, its cool intrusion dragging her back to reality, dissolving her wistful dreams of Simon and a romantic world that no longer existed. "Remember me? We met at breakfast this morning. At our hotel. I was there with my husband Tom and our baby daughter Gracie."

Annabel turned slowly, reluctant to let the warm memories fade away.

"Oh…hi, Tessa. Sorry…I was miles away."

Tessa laughed, her blond curls bobbing. "Venice affects people like that." She glanced over her shoulder at her baby daughter, fast asleep in a sling attached to her back. "I, um…look, since I've found you, could I ask a special favor?"

"Sure," Annabel said, but her heart gave a tiny jump. She had a feeling the favor had something to do with Tessa's baby, and anything to do with babies, especially baby girls, still brought a painful tremor, a tightening in her chest. "What can I do?"

"Could you hold Gracie for me, just for a few minutes, while I try on a dress? I've just fed her, so she should stay asleep." The rest came out in a breathless rush. "We've a special dinner tomorrow night—my husband's here for an orthopedics conference—and I've seen this fantastic dress in a boutique window just up the next lane. I'd love to try it on, but Gracie—"

"I'd be happy to look after her," Annabel said, try-ing to sound as if she meant it. She *did* mean it. She loved babies. It was just that she hadn't held a baby since the traumatic day she'd lost her precious daugh-ter. Even now, she could feel her body shaking, her heart squeezing at the agonizing memory.

"Oh, thank you, you're an angel!" Tessa was al-ready tugging her away, dodging the tourists swarm-ing along the famous sweeping promenade known as the *Riva degli Schiavoni,* before dragging her into a nearby lane. "You must have dinner with us tonight at the hotel, Annabel, Tom has a free evening, no confer-ence commitments. Please say you will. It's my way of saying thank you."

"You don't need to thank me, but…all right, I'd love to," she said. Tessa and Tom were a bright, friendly couple, and spending an evening with them might give her something else to think about than Simon and…all that she'd lost.

"Great! Let's meet in the dining room at seven-thirty." By now, they were halfway along the bustling lane. Tessa paused outside an upmarket boutique. "The dress is in this window. See? Isn't it divine? They may even have others equally as fantastic that I could try on…" She looked hopefully at Annabel.

"You take your time. Give Gracie to me," Annabel said, steeling her heart for the ordeal ahead. "Here. I'll help you undo the sling. I'll do my best not to wake her."

"Thanks. If she does stir, just take her for a walk. That should do the trick. St. Mark's Square is just along a bit, round the corner. If she stays awake, she'd love to see the pigeons."

"No worries," said Annabel, worrying regardless. As she helped Tessa transfer Gracie onto her own back, just the sweet smell of the sleeping baby was playing havoc with her senses, bringing back nostalgic, heartbreaking memories of her precious one-year-old daughter. Lily would have been three years old by now.

How Annabel missed her! Before succumbing to the flu and pneumonia, she'd been able to bury the worst of her grief in her work, taking on more and more demanding assignments to blot out the unbearable agony of her private heartbreak. But since her illness had forced her to take several weeks off work, she'd had the time, finally, to think and grieve, and she was missing Lily more than ever.

It made her realize—especially now that she was back in Venice—how much she'd been missing Simon, too. Maybe coming here had been a mistake. Dredging up memories of Simon and happier times was hardly likely to help her recovery. She didn't want to think of Simon! In all this time—nearly two years—she hadn't seen or heard a word from him. He hadn't cared enough about her even to make inquiries about her…let alone seek her out and maybe even begin to forgive her.

She flinched as a piercing stab of pain revived other hurtful memories. Simon had barely been able to speak to her, or even to look her in the eye, in the weeks before she'd walked out on him. His neurosurgery demands and his patients had been his only solace, his only escape. Though he'd never accused her to her face, she knew he blamed her for Lily's death, and he still blamed her, obviously, or he would have come after her long before now. And she *was* to blame. Her blind trust, her slow reactions, had been responsible for the loss of their beloved baby daughter. She still had nightmares about that speeding car…visions of her baby's pram flying into the air…

Tessa's baby whimpered, jolting her back to her present dilemma. "I'd better go for that walk," she said, and swung away, leaving Tessa to her evening gowns. Thankfully, the baby quickly drifted back to sleep under the rhythmic movement of her swaying stride.

Crossing St. Mark's Square, Venice's famous piazza, was as exhilarating as it always was, despite the crowds of tourists who loved to flock there and get in the way. Every speck of space in that huge square seemed to be taken up with people or pigeons, the pigeons so thick on the ground and so tame they barely fluttered into the air when intruders threatened their space.

Annabel tried to ignore the crowds by looking beyond them, admiring the arcaded buildings on either side, lined with expensive jewelry shops, boutiques and cafés. At the far end of the square she could see the towering brick bell tower—the *Campanile*, as the Italians called it—and the Byzantine splendor of the glorious, dominating Basilica, with its bulbous domes and the four bronze horses of St. Mark looking ready to prance off the grand facade.

The trouble was, seeing the Basilica made her think of Simon again. They'd explored the impressive building together four years ago, but there'd been almost too much magnificence to take in at one visit and they'd vowed to meet up again one day and come back for another look.

But she'd found herself pregnant instead, which had changed everything, opening up a whole new life for both of them. A life they'd shared happily and chaotically with their baby daughter…until it had ended suddenly, tragically.

Now she was back in Venice…alone. She felt the hot sting of tears and resolutely blinked them away. As her eyes cleared, her gaze settled on a group of white-clothed outdoor tables, mostly unoccupied. And no wonder, she thought with a rueful half smile. Few tourists could afford even to sit down at Caffè Florian's elite tables, let alone to buy the famous café's astronomically expensive coffee.

But one dark-haired man obviously could. He was sitting alone, lounging back as if it were the most natural thing in the world to indulge in outrageously expensive coffee at Florian's.

Something about him, as he watched a pigeon land at his feet, made her eyes snap wide and sent her heart to her throat. The strongly carved profile, the familiar shape of his head, the thick dark hair curling over his ears, the imposing breadth of his shoulders…

No! She tried to blink the disturbing image away. It was impossible! Was she going to see Simon Pacino in every dark-haired, good-looking hunk she came across in Venice just because she'd met him here once before?

And then he glanced up, turned and looked straight at her, his gaze boring through the milling crowd as if only she existed. Dear heaven, it *was* Simon!

She nearly tripped, but managed somehow to keep on walking, still not believing it, her mind scattering in panic. How could he be here, of all the places in the world he could have chosen…that *she* had chosen, too? Coincidences like this just didn't happen. Besides, he was still back in Sydney…wasn't he? Or had he left the hospital where he'd been working—the hospital that must hold so many painful memories for him—and moved overseas himself? Maybe…maybe he'd hitched up with someone new and was waiting for her to join him.

Oh God…

She had to put distance between them!

With a nonchalance she was far from feeling, determined not to give way to panic, she veered sideways, forcing her legs to carry her to the far side of the square, well away from Florian's elegant tables, before turning and making her way back in the direction she'd come from. Tempted as she was to break into a run she resisted the urge, partly to avoid jolting baby Gracie awake, but mostly to avoid attracting attention. *Simon's* attention.

Maybe he hadn't recognized her. It was almost two years since he'd last seen her, and she wore her deep auburn hair short these days, in a smooth, head-hugging bob, with a few golden highlights to brighten it up. He'd only ever seen it long, falling over her shoulders in thick russet waves, or swept back in a ponytail. He'd loved to run his fingers through her hair—one of the reasons she'd cut it.

She'd also lost a lot of weight recently, due to her illness. Even before she'd fallen sick, she'd shed weight, too busy most of the time to eat properly and barely interested in food anyway.

"Excuse me."

She felt a hand on her shoulder and knew instantly

whose hand it was. Light as the touch was, could any other hand have this instant, electrifying effect on her, scalding her skin through her thin layer of clothing and sending shuddering shock waves through her body?

She turned, deliberately slowly, masking her features as she tried to still her wildly fluttering heart. Compelling blue eyes, sharpened by the sun, devoured her tense face.

"It *is* you." He spoke in a quiet, velvet-edged tone, showing no visible surprise, as if they were old acquaintances who hadn't seen each other in a while, who'd never suffered a common pain and grief, who'd never grown apart until there was nothing left between them. At the time she'd walked out on him, he'd barely been speaking to her, his eyes flat and remote whenever they'd come into close contact, a man in torment, coldly shutting her out, holding back the words of blame and anger he must have longed to hurl at her.

Now, two years later, his face was deeply bronzed, accentuating the intense blue of his eyes, and he looked amazingly toned and fit. How had he managed to get so tanned and superfit when he worked such long days, and often nights, too, in a brightly lit operating room? Did his hospital have a gym now, with suntanning facilities?

She felt his piercing gaze sear over her face, her hair, her far-too-thin body. "You look different," he said. "Different, yet…just the same."

"I'm far from the same." She spoke sharply, unable to keep a tinge of bitterness from her voice. Oh yes, she was different. More battle-hardened, more in control of her emotions and her life, more determined than ever to reach her ultimate goal—a partnership in her highly respected law firm, which was all she had to look forward to now.

His dark-lashed blue eyes veered to the baby in the sling. They flared for a second, then died. "Yes...so I see." The cold remoteness she'd last seen two years ago was back in force. "You didn't waste any time replacing your child...or your lover."

His scorn lashed her in two. Stung, she lashed back. "I see time hasn't changed *you* in the least." He was still as coldly distant and unfeeling as he'd been when she walked out on him two years ago. The realization brought an odd quiver of regret. Feeling the effect his touch still had on her, she'd hoped for a second...

Stupid of her. Futile. Nothing could ever heal the bitter scars of the past, could ever bring them back together...not after all they'd been through.

"I have to go," she said bleakly. "I have someone to meet."

"Your lover?" This time he caught her arm with just enough force to prevent her from walking off without having to forcibly break free. There was something else in his eyes now, a dangerous glint in the icy depths. *Anger.* A cold, deadly anger. "He can't be your husband. We're still married. You've never sought a divorce."

Neither had he, but she didn't say it. "Marriage isn't high on my list of priorities anymore," she said, her voice tight. She'd never even considered divorce, knowing she'd never want to marry again—or, at least, never want to marry any other man. Though if *he'd* demanded a divorce...

"No...it never was, was it?" His own voice held a

note of weary resignation, though his broad shoulders were stiff with tension, as if that icy anger still simmered below.

She recoiled at the harsh words, hurt piercing her at the reminder that they'd only married because he'd made her pregnant, the legacy of their last rapturous night together in Venice four years ago. It was something they hadn't expected would happen, naively hoping it wouldn't happen after only that one time…even after finding that the condom he'd used that night had split.

Attracted as they'd been to each other, they'd been virtual strangers at the time, both immersed in their high-powered careers, blazing ambition driving them equally—she striving to reach the top of her field in a male-dominated corporate law firm, he determined to be the best in his own demanding field of neurosurgery. Neither had been ready for marriage or commitment, let alone children. Finding herself pregnant after returning to Sydney from Venice had come as a shock. She'd only called Simon because she'd needed someone to confide in after making the difficult decision to keep the baby. Even though he was working in New York at the time, she'd felt it was right that he, as the child's father, be aware of the situation.

"You only married me because I insisted on coming back to Australia and giving our child a name and two married parents," the deep, relentless voice went on. "I'm not even sure you would have gone ahead and *had* the baby if I hadn't persuaded you to marry me."

She jerked back, horrified that he could believe such a thing. Her heart cried out to him. *No! I'd already fallen in love with you, Simon, even though we barely knew each other!* Having already decided to keep the baby by then, she'd hoped he *would* stand by her, though it had come as a shock when he'd asked her to marry him. That had been the last thing she'd expected, after what he'd said in Venice about not being ready for marriage or children, wanting to reach the top of his specialized field before settling down. After *she'd* said the same thing. She'd hesitated at first, but when he'd refused to take no for an answer, she'd surprised herself by agreeing to marry him, knowing in her heart, after only that short time together in Venice, that she'd found the man she wanted to spend the rest of her life with.

Simon had been her rock back then. He'd given up his work at the hospital in New York and returned to Sydney to be with her, taking up a post at a top Sydney hospital. He'd supported her through her pregnancy and made it possible for her to keep on working after the baby arrived. A daily nanny and a housekeeper twice a week had allowed them both to keep on working at the same frenetic pace, each determined not to allow a baby, even a much loved baby, to disrupt their high-flying ambitions.

Now, forcing herself to look into his eyes—coldly glinting and remote as they were—she said evenly, "There was never any question of not having the baby, once I knew I was pregnant. I—I would have managed somehow." But as a struggling single mother, what would have happened to her lofty hopes of a partnership and a brilliantly successful career at the top of her elite field? And oh, how her father, back in Queensland, would have crowed as it all crashed down around her! *I told you you'd never make it. Careers are for men, love, not for women. Women belong in the home. Mothers belong at home with their children.*

"But you didn't have to manage on your own, did you?" Simon reminded her tonelessly. His hand had dropped to his side. "I flew back from New York and we got married. But marriage didn't change your life, did it, Annabel? Having a baby didn't change anything. You didn't even change your name. Your career still came first. Never our marriage." Or *me,* he might as well have added.

She almost moaned aloud. How could she dispute it? But she hadn't been the only one obsessed with a demanding career. "It didn't change your life, either," she reminded him. "We both messed up big time. Neither of us was ready for marriage." Or for babies, she thought, feeling the old hollow pain inside. But she wasn't brave enough to mention Lily. Since the accident, neither of them had been able to talk about their daughter…least of all Simon. And here in crowded St. Mark's Square certainly wasn't the time or place.

"No." Simon puffed out a sigh. "And marriage is still not a priority with you…obviously." He glanced again at the sleeping baby nestled against her. "But having another child *is?*" This time he didn't hide the bitterness, the raw pain in his voice. "Or was this one a mistake, too? Where *is* the father, by the way? Did he hang around? Or have you had to manage on your own this time?"

The baby started making whimpering sounds, and Annabel, losing her nerve, seized her chance to make a run for it. Let him think what he liked…it was over between them. Nothing could ever change what had happened or repair the damage from the past. Or make him love her again. "I must go. What I do is no longer any of your business."

"You're still my wife." His hand caught her arm again, his fingers scalding her bare skin, his intense blue eyes far too close, burning into hers.

She felt another surge of panic. "We're separated. I'm free to see any man I please."

"Separated!" He made a sound that was almost a snarl. "We never even discussed it. You just walked out. No warning, no discussion, nothing."

She turned on him. "You're pretending to *care* now?"

He flinched. "And you did? It didn't seem that way when you left without a word, except for a brief Dear John letter saying our marriage was over and you were leaving Australia to work in London. You couldn't even face me. You didn't explain…or ask for any help…for a settlement…for anything. You just cut me out of your life."

She steeled her heart, holding herself together with an effort. "I didn't need anything from you. We were both financially independent. Our marriage was dead. What was the point in going on?"

His hand slid away. "No…you never needed anything from me, did you? Not after…" His voice cracked.

He still couldn't say Lily's name. Since the day their baby had died, he hadn't even been able to talk about her, let alone discuss what had happened. Annabel felt the old anguish, the deep, suffocating hurt of two years ago, swell in her throat. He was still suffering from

what *she* had done. Still blaming her. What hope did
they have? Blinking, she swung away, plunging into the
crowd, scattering pigeons as she left him standing.

Chapter Two

Good grief, what have I done to her? Scowling at the fluttering pigeons, Simon trudged back across the crowded square, his heart twisting with guilt and self-loathing.

Oh, Annabel... Still as beautiful, as desirable as ever, but so thin and pale, the lovely green eyes smudged and clouded with pain, her cheekbones too stark, a shadow of her old vibrant self. Even at the time she'd walked out on him, she hadn't looked as frail as this.

Of course, she'd been sick. She'd had pneumonia, her secretary had told him last week when he'd finally taken the bit between his teeth and called Annabel's London office to inquire about her. But *he'd* started her on her downward slide, crushing her last desperate hope, breaking her heart and spirit. He'd wrecked her life, as he'd wrecked...their child's. As well as his own, for what it was worth.

Damn damn damn. He'd thought that after this long healing break away from each other, and by taking the plunge finally and pursuing her to Venice, where they'd first fallen for each other, she might have been prepared to thaw a little and feel more forgiving, maybe even give him another chance. But he'd come back for her too late. She'd found someone else. She'd even had another man's child!

He groaned aloud. How the hell had she been managing, working long demanding hours in a strange city, and having to care for a baby? The guy *must* still be with her. Some wealthy, high-powered legal hotshot, no doubt, who was supporting not only her and their baby, but her dream of a partnership in her prestigious law firm. A man who could give her everything she'd ever wanted.

Not a broken-down brain surgeon like himself.

He swore. What a humiliating comedown! From a stunningly successful neurosurgeon, brimming with self-confidence and his own lofty importance, treated almost like a god who could do no wrong, he'd sunk to this. A failure—despite what others might have tried to tell him. His pride and his confidence had taken a beating, but that was nothing compared to what else he'd lost. His child, his wife, his marriage.

He shouldered his way through a Japanese tour group clustered round a guide with a yellow umbrella, barely seeing them, only knowing they were in his way. He could only see Annabel. His *wife*. The thought of her making love to another man was like a knife twisting in his gut.

Who *was* he, this jerk who'd come between them?

A close colleague at her London law firm, as likely as not, knowing how hard she worked and how determined she was to reach her longed-for goal. Maybe even a senior partner at Mallaby's. What better, quicker way to achieve her coveted ambition?

Unless they'd made her a partner already. The legal secretary he'd spoken to had not been communicative. It had taken all his charm and persuasion just to find out that Annabel had been ill and was recuperating in Venice.

"Well! Simon Pacino! I don't believe it!"

The tormenting images in his mind disintegrated as a vaguely familiar face materialized out of the crowd. The sandy hair...the cocky grin...the short, stout body...

"Remember me, mate? Tom Robson. We were at med school together in Melbourne. Many moons ago, before you moved to Sydney and we lost touch."

The years rolled back. "Tom! Of course I remember. You planned to specialize in orthopedics."

"And you in neurosurgery."

They both gave a laugh, a chopped-off laugh, eyeing each other as if wary of asking if the other had achieved his goal.

"You didn't change your mind?" Simon asked finally, getting in first as he prepared his own answer in his mind. The fewer details, the better. It was no one's business but...Annabel's. If she wanted to hear. And if he had the chance to open up to her...finally. And *could* open up, spill his guts, lay himself bare. Hell! Why was exposing his darkest feelings and private hells always so damned difficult for him?

"No way," said Tom. "I'm considered a top ortho-pedic surgeon these days." False modesty had never been Tom's way. "I work in Chicago now, by the way. I'm here in Venice to give a presentation at an ortho-pedics convention." He glanced at his watch. "Look, I have to rush off now, but how about joining us for din-ner? My wife's here with me and we've a free night. We could catch up on everything then."

Everything? *I don't think so.* Simon hesitated, searching for an excuse. He wanted—needed—to be at a particular hotel tonight…to look out for Annabel. An-nabel and her…lover.

"We're staying at the Gabrielli Sandwirth, on the Lagoon." Tom was already backing away. "Say you'll join us. Seven-thirty in the dining-room? Hope that's not too early? We've a new baby and my wife prefers early nights."

Another baby? Simon groaned inwardly. Just what he needed. More reminders of…

"Congratulations, Tom." He mouthed the platitude while his mind was racing off at a tangent, having seized on the name of the hotel. *The Gabrielli Sandwirth*…the very hotel where Annabel was staying! He'd spent all morning checking out the hotels until he found out. An-nabel's secretary wouldn't divulge that information when he'd called London, only relenting enough to mention that she was in Venice. Learning she'd already left the hotel for the day, he'd hung around St. Mark's Square in the hope of finding her. And by some mira-cle, she'd shown up there. With a *baby*. He grimaced.

"I'll be there," he promised, his mind on his wife, not on meeting up again with Tom. Dining at the Gabrielli with other people would give him some cover if Annabel walked in with…lover boy. If she walked in alone—he sent up a silent prayer—he'd excuse himself as soon as he could and join her…if she would let him. He wasn't going to give her up without a fight, without thrashing things out…not this time. He'd already lost her once.

And he would lose her again if he couldn't face up to his demons and deal with them.

"Great. See you tonight, mate." Flashing a broad grin, Tom strode off.

Simon had a satisfied smile on his lips and almost a skip in his step as he walked on. Dinner at the Gabrielli? What a stroke of luck. He would have to see if the hotel had a spare room. If they did, he'd retrieve his bag from the railway station and move in there. Annabel was still married to him and, new lover or not, baby or not, he was damned well going to win her back and convince her they *could* make it work. Somehow. He had nothing to lose.

Hell, he'd lost enough already.

Annabel came down to the dining room early, not wanting to keep Tessa and Tom waiting. But only Tom was there, at a table set for four. Four? Oh well, she hoped that whoever else they'd invited would keep the conversation rolling, because she didn't feel like being the life of the party herself. She was weary after sightseeing all day and emotionally drained after bumping into Simon.

"Annabel! Glad you could join us. Tessa's just feeding the baby. She'll be down in a minute." Tom settled her into a chair. "We owe you for what you did for Tessa this afternoon. She's bankrupted me, but hey, she tried on her new dress for me and she looked a dream. She'll knock everyone's eyes out tomorrow night."

He chatted on easily until Tessa arrived, carrying a portable crib. "Gracie's been well fed and is fast asleep already," she said, slipping into the chair beside her husband and placing the baby capsule on the floor beside her. "Now we should be able to have dinner without being disturbed."

"Ah, and here's Simon," said Tom, raising his arm.

Annabel glanced round, expecting to see a fellow delegate of Tom's from his orthopedics conference. She froze, her eyes flaring in shocked dismay. The last person she'd expected to see was Simon Pacino! How did *Tom* know him?

As Simon's gaze flicked to hers, she saw her own shock mirrored in the blue of his eyes—only maybe without the same dismay. More surprise, bemusement, than dismay.

"You already know each other?" Tom eyed them uncertainly—maybe because of their obvious shock and the fact that neither was smiling.

"We met earlier today, in St. Mark's Square," came Annabel's quick reply. "By accident."

"We knew each other back in Australia," Simon said deliberately. "Only we lost touch. She's living in London now."

Annabel tensed, willing him not to say more. He didn't...for the time being, at least.

"Well...old friends. That's great." Tom, sensing some tension, didn't push it. "This is my wife Tessa," he said, resting a hand on his wife's shoulder.

Simon, summoning his familiar lopsided smile for the first time—a smile that twisted Annabel's heart, making her wonder if he'd ever again smile like that for her—skirted the table to shake Tessa's hand. "And this must be...your new baby," he said when he saw the baby beside her.

Annabel held her breath. Had Simon recognized the baby from this afternoon? Fast asleep and bundled up in different blankets, with only her tiny face visible, would he be able to tell?

"Our baby daughter Gracie," Tom said proudly from behind. "Take a seat, Simon. Here, between the two ladies."

As the men settled into their places, Annabel gulped in some much needed breaths of air. Was Simon wondering where *her* baby was? And where her so-called lover was? Any minute now, she expected him to ask if her baby's father would be joining them—or if he was remaining upstairs to babysit while she was down here socializing! Husbands and wives often did cooperate that way. Wistfully, she recalled the evenings when she'd had a legal function or dinner meeting to attend and Simon had babysat Lily. Or the evenings when she'd minded Lily while he was operating throughout the night. Busy as they'd both been, mutual give-and-take had made their marriage work.

A marriage without a lasting, solid base...as time had shown.

Oh, this was a nightmare! How was she going to survive dinner, making polite conversation with an estranged husband who thought she was tied up with another man and already had a new baby? An unplanned baby...

History repeating itself, he must be thinking, and hating her for it. But then, he hated her already. In their last painful weeks together, even on the few occasions they'd had sex, there'd been no comforting words of love, no whispers of forgiveness or understanding, none of the old intimacy they'd once shared. Not since he'd lost his precious Lily. *Her* precious Lily, too…

"Well, this is amazing," Tom said, rather too jovially. "Fancy all of us meeting up here in Venice, after all this time! Simon and I studied medicine together, you know. We were at Melbourne Uni together, and haven't seen each other since. We both have lots to catch up on. But first, tell us about yourself, Annabel. What brings you to Venice?"

The last thing she wanted was for the focus to be on her. Luckily, the arrival of a drink waiter gave her a moment's reprieve, a chance to put her chaotic thoughts in some sort of order. As they ordered drinks, she could feel Simon's eyes boring into her face, sense him waiting for her answer.

"Okay, Annabel," said Tom, after they'd raised their glasses and sipped dutifully. "You have the floor."

She managed a smile, urging herself to keep her answer light and brief. "I've had time off work with pneumonia," she said. "I'm better now, but my law firm refused to let me come back until I took a short break away from London. The weather's been really foul there lately." She shrugged. "That's about it. The minute I heard it was sunny and warm in Venice, I headed here."

Maybe she'd been searching for something more than just sun and warmth. Redemption, maybe. Peace. Hoping that the memories of her first visit to Venice, when she and Simon had met and had such a blissful time together, might have given some balm to her soul, reminding her that they'd been happy together...once. She needed some happy memories...not only of their carefree romance in Venice, but happy memories of their daughter, too...memories of the short, beautiful time they'd had her. Memories to cherish.

So much for finding peace or salvation in sunny Venice! Simon's unexpected arrival and the hostile confrontation that had followed had shattered any soothing calm she might have found here. Stung by his bitter attack on her, she'd let him believe his ready assumption that she'd found another man...that she'd had another man's *baby*, for heaven's sake. As if they didn't have enough *real* issues to deal with!

"You didn't bring *your* baby with you, Annabel?" Simon asked her, his gaze pinning hers so that she could catch the ominous glint in his eye.

Her heart dipped. He wanted to confront her *now*, in front of Tessa and Tom? He'd be asking her about her phantom lover next! If they'd been alone, she might have been tempted to string out the elaborate fiction a bit longer, as a self-protective mechanism, but with witnesses here, she knew she would have to come clean.

"Baby?" Tessa looked at her in confusion.

Annabel sighed, resigned to the inevitable, but needing to take another quick breath before answering. She didn't want to talk about babies, fictitious or otherwise. It might lead to painful revelations about her own lost baby. *Our* baby, she corrected herself, sliding another veiled glance at Simon. He wouldn't say anything about their daughter if she didn't.

"The baby you saw me with this afternoon was Tessa's." Her voice caught a little, as it always did when she had to say the word *baby.* "I was minding Gracie while Tessa did some shopping." She waved a hand in the direction of the sleeping baby in the capsule on the floor. "Didn't you recognize her?" she asked, trying to make light of it, even managing a teasing note.

She was relieved when Simon's gaze swiveled round, away from *her.* "Babies look different when they're hidden in blankets, fast asleep," was all he said. If he felt any anger at her subterfuge, or any triumph at her forced confession—or any relief—he wasn't showing it, his tone coolly impassive.

She drew in another fractured breath. *At least he hadn't said, All babies look alike.* But then Simon wouldn't. Not after having a baby daughter of his own. *Losing* a much loved baby of his own. Emotion welled up inside her, and she grabbed at the menu like a lifeline.

Even with her nose buried in the menu, she could feel Simon's probing gaze on her. Finally, risking a glance up, ready to defy any condemnation she saw in his eyes, she was surprised to see a glimmer of concern in the piercing blue, when he had good reason to be gloating at catching her out. She felt a shivery tremor run through her.

"Well, what are we going to have to eat?" Tom asked cheerily, and the awkward moment passed.

Over their meal, Tom kept the conversational ball rolling with tales of knee operations and amputated legs, and how he'd met Tessa while she was working as a physiotherapist and how he'd proposed to her within weeks. By the time their dessert arrived, the wine had loosened Tom's tongue enough for him to risk getting personal again and quizzing Simon about *his* life.

"Enough about us...tell us about *your* brilliant career, Simon. I don't doubt it *has* been brilliant. You were always so determined to be the best in your field one day. You must be a top neurosurgeon by now."

"Actually, I gave up neurosurgery eighteen months ago," came the cool response. As Annabel's head snapped back in shock, Simon, in the same impassive tone, explained. "I damaged my hand and couldn't operate. I worked as a neurologist while I was having treatment, then took a year off to sail around the world."

The room spun. Annabel couldn't believe what she was hearing. Simon, the dedicated, hardworking neurosurgeon, unable to operate? Being forced to give up neurosurgery? Her heart went out to him. It was the only thing he'd ever wanted to do. He'd devoted his life to it.

She'd once asked him why he'd decided on neurosurgery, wondering what had motivated such a demanding choice of career. Knowing little about him at the time, she'd assumed it must have been the money, or the prestige, or even a secret passion for fancy cars and the good life. But his answer, when it eventually came, had shown he hadn't done it for himself at all.

"My mother died of a brain tumor. The doctors couldn't save her, even though it was operable." He'd shown no emotion, no anger, no resentment, clearly well-practiced at hiding his feelings. "We couldn't afford the best neurosurgeon...we had to make do with the specialist chosen for us. He was...inexperienced and inadequate. I swore the day my mother died that I was going to study medicine when I finished school, then specialize in neurosurgery and become the top brain surgeon in the country. It was too late for my mother," he'd added heavily, "but hopefully I could help others with a similar need for the best skills and care."

And he'd succeeded brilliantly, despite the fact that he'd had to do it entirely on his own. His father had walked out on his family when Simon was only seven, and he'd had no brothers or sisters or other family support. He'd never given her a reason for his father leaving home, always withdrawing and closing up when she asked about that obviously painful time in his life.

Simon had always found it hard to open up, even to her, she mused with a tug of regret. He'd kept his emotions and past hurts locked away somewhere deep inside him. Even when Lily died, at a time when she'd most needed his support, and he'd most needed hers, he'd shut himself off from her. She'd known he was silently condemning her for what had happened to Lily, for letting the accident happen—just as she'd blamed herself, and still did. He'd thrown himself even deeper into his demanding surgical work, the one thing left that meant something to him. That meant *everything*.

And now, apparently, he'd lost that, too

She ran sympathetic eyes over his right hand as it curled round his wine glass, then over his other hand resting on the table—the hands she'd once longed to feel on her body—noting the long, sensitive surgeon's fingers that had healed so many. Both hands looked fine to her. As they must be by now if he'd been able to sail around the world for the past year.

Sail! She'd never known Simon to sail a boat before.

She had so much she wanted to ask him! But she could sense him retreating again, could read the signs she'd come to know so well. And perhaps it was just as well. She didn't want to ask him personal questions in front of Tom and Tessa, two people she barely knew. Yet she did want to ask him…sometime. Which meant she would have to see him again.

But would he want to see *her?*

"So…what have you all seen of Venice so far?" Leaning back in his chair, Simon deftly changed the subject, shifting the focus away from himself. As he'd been doing from the day she'd first met him, she thought wistfully, seldom opening up fully, never telling her more than he thought she needed to know. Or more than he *wanted* her to know.

She had a feeling there was something in his past— long before she'd met him—that was secretly tormenting him, and she suspected it might have something to do with his father, who'd walked out on his family when Simon was barely seven years old. She remembered asking him once if he'd ever tried to seek out his father, a man he hadn't seen or heard of in all the years since, and his answer had been harsh and unequivocal. "No, and I never will. My father is dead as far as I'm concerned."

Simon, when badly hurt by something, or somebody, could be a closed, hard, unforgiving man, she'd concluded sadly when he'd shut *her* out as well after Lily died.

Tom and Tessa, sensing Simon's reluctance to talk

about his changed circumstances and loath to probe any deeper, leapt at the chance to talk about Venice's many attractions. Soon they were all talking at once, swapping notes and suggesting places the others simply must see.

The magic of Venice had come to the rescue. Just as Simon, diving into the Grand Canal like a wildly romantic, heroic Italian Romeo, had come to *her* rescue once, Annabel mused, a pensive smile curving her lips.

Simon saw Annabel's smile and wondered if she was thinking back, too, remembering the day they'd first met, when she'd fallen overboard and he'd jumped into the Grand Canal to save her, sweeping her into his arms and pulling her out of the water…a flowing-haired, dripping water-nymph with the most wondrous green eyes he'd ever seen.

A touch of cynicism quirked his lip. It was more likely she was wondering why he was here *now* and how she could avoid seeing any more of him. She'd already tried her best to get rid of him by letting him believe she'd had another man's child. Thank God, it hadn't been true. If he hadn't reacted so violently to seeing her with a strange baby, hadn't hurled those bitter accusations at her, maybe she would have told him the truth from the start.

Now that they'd both had time to cool down a bit and at least had *that* complication out of the way, he'd be wise to curb his impatience and give her time to adjust to having him back in her life. Or if not *in her life*, at least to seeing more of him.

He had to stop her turning away from him again, running off again without even making an effort to resolve what had gone wrong between them. If it meant avoiding any ràsh confrontations or sore points for the time being and just enjoying each other again, the way they'd managed to do four years ago, he'd damned well do his best to curb his impatience. Gaining her trust again, her confidence, was top priority and he mustn't rush things and risk wrecking everything.

And regaining her love? Would that be possible as well? Or was it too late for that?

He recalled the shocked concern in her eyes when he'd announced that he'd injured his hand and given up neurosurgery. It gave him a flare of hope. Maybe she still felt something for him. She'd always encouraged him in his career, as he'd supported hers. The thought that she could feel some concern for him now, after what his so-called surgical skills had done to their lives, to their precious daughter, was like a glimmer of sunlight through dark clouds.

And what about her brilliant legal career? He hoped her recent illness hadn't jeopardized her chances of a partnership, after she'd worked so hard to reach her cherished goal, assuming she hadn't achieved it already. She'd given away nothing about her current status at work over dinner, and he hadn't wanted to ask in front of Tom and Tessa. He needed to be alone with her, to find out everything she'd been doing in the past two years.

When she was ready… He'd be mad to put any pressure on her. She'd already run away from him once…he didn't want to lose her again.

At a thin cry from the baby in the capsule, Tessa pushed back her chair. "I think Gracie's ready for a change of nappy…and maybe another feed. Would you mind if I called it a night? Tom, you stay and have coffee…"

But Tom was already on his feet. "I'll come with you. I've some notes to look at before tomorrow…"

"Time I went, too," Annabel said at once, rising swiftly to her feet as a rush of nervous tension gripped her. Despite all the questions she longed to ask Simon, particularly about his injured hand and his disrupted career, she wasn't sure she could handle being alone with him just yet. Especially not late in the evening, in romantic, moonlit Venice…

Tomorrow, perhaps…in more calming daylight…if he wanted to see more of *her*.

She saw a dark eyebrow rise ever so slightly as Simon stood up, too, but other than that he showed no reaction, no trace of the disappointment she'd expected—or perhaps had hoped—to see. It threw her a bit, making her conscious of a contrary sense of pique. If he pressed her to stay, or even invited her to join him for an evening stroll along the *Riva,* she wasn't sure she would have the willpower to resist.

"Have you been back to the Basilica yet?" he asked her, and she paused, her heart picking up a beat. Was he remembering the vow they'd made four years ago?

"I've only seen it from the outside. I was thinking of going there in the morning before the queue grows too long." She spoke carelessly, glancing away to hide any hint of an invitation in her eyes. He'd hurt her badly in the last weeks of their marriage and she wasn't going to easily fall back into his arms, if that was what he was hoping. Her heart couldn't bear any more hurt.

"I had the same idea," he said in a similar offhand tone, with no sign of a suggestive glint in his eye as she flicked her gaze back to his. At one time, there would have been a distinct roguish twinkle evident. She wondered pensively if he'd lost it forever.

"If you've no objection to some company," he was quick to add. "I'll get there well before the doors open at nine-thirty and hold a spot for you at the front of the queue. That'll give you a chance to sleep in a bit and not rush your breakfast."

He'd always been considerate that way, she remembered with a bittersweet pang. At least, until the tragedy of Lily's death had changed him, turning him into a closed, distant stranger.

"Let's just play it by ear," she said, keeping her tone light. "Is your hotel far from here?" she asked, expecting him to head for the lobby, while she took the lift up to her room.

The firm, well-shaped lips she'd always found so irresistible—and still did, she realized with a tremor—eased into the familiar curved smile she'd thought lost forever, at least to her. Seeing it again gave her spirits a lift. "Actually, I'm staying here," he said. "Fourth floor. We can ride up in the lift together."

She almost missed her step. It was the last thing she'd expected to hear. Staying *here?* On the floor above hers? Maybe his room, his *bed*, were directly over hers. How would she ever be able to sleep, knowing he was so close to her, just a few floorboards separating them?

"After you," he said, his voice sounding dangerously seductive all of a sudden.

As she stepped into the empty lift ahead of him, she

realized that his room on the fourth floor was the least of her worries. The walls of the tiny lift seemed to close in on her as he followed her in, standing far too close, filling the small space with his tall, potent presence, surrounding her with his familiar male scent, the heady warmth of his breath.

Inwardly, she felt herself gasping for air, clutching for normality and reason. They were only sharing a lift, for heaven's sake.

Maybe it was her heightened imagination, but it seemed to take an age to reach the first floor, another age to reach the second, and finally, with her heart thumping so loudly by then she was sure he must hear it, the lift doors swung open.

"Good night, Simon!" Her voice was a ragged gasp as she lurched out without looking back.

So much for acting cool! She'd failed dismally, and now he'd know she wasn't indifferent to him. He'd been indifferent to *her* for so long, withholding the love and warmth he'd once shown for her, that she should be guarding her heart a whole lot better than this.

Chapter Three

Despite barely sleeping a wink all night, Annabel didn't sleep in. Instead, she rose early and dived straight into the shower. She both dreaded and longed to see Simon again, fearing how things might turn out, yet hoping desperately that some life still glimmered in the ashes of their marriage.

There was a basket of fresh fruit in her room and she ate a banana and an apple instead of going down to the dining room for breakfast, not wanting to face anyone before spending some time alone with Simon. She felt confused about so many things and wanted answers that only Simon could give her in private.

When she did finally leave her room she avoided the lift and slipped down the stairs to the lobby, pausing only to leave a note in Tessa's mailbox before hurrying from the hotel.

The crisp air and the silvery early morning sunlight jolted her fully awake as she scurried along the *Riva* toward St. Mark's Square. Hordes of tourists were already disembarking from boats and swarming along the promenade in the same direction. She hoped they weren't all rushing to queue up at the Basilica.

Was Simon already there at the head of the queue, or had a boatload of tourists beaten him to it and already crowded in front of him? She felt a smile twitching her lips. He'd never had much tolerance for crowds. Or for waiting around doing nothing, for that matter.

As she passed the pink marble walls and lace-like arcades of the Doge's Palace, she saw a long queue snaking from the Basilica, and groaned. That long *already?* It was barely eight-thirty—an hour before opening time!

And then she saw Simon, standing close to the decorative arched doorway at the very head of the queue. Heavens, he must have been here at dawn!

She felt a twinge of guilt that she hadn't come even earlier to keep him company. An American tour group had gathered behind him, led by a flag-wielding female who was striding back and forth shouting facts about the Basilica to keep her flock amused. Annabel braved their stares as she strode up to Simon, her cheeks pink with embarrassment.

"I feel as if I'm pushing in," she whispered, ready to slink away. But Simon's smile—a *real* smile for the first time, even reaching his eyes, those incredibly blue eyes—stopped her in her tracks. He'd always been sexy as the devil, with the height and bearing to make him stand out in any crowd. But with that heart-stopping smile, his deeply bronzed skin enhancing the blue of his eyes, his longer hair and the casual denim jacket and jeans that he wore so easily, he was a sight to snatch a girl's breath away.

"They'll see we're together, so don't even think about running off," he growled, reaching for her arm and pulling her closer.

She glanced down at the tanned hand circling her arm. It was his right hand…the skilled, sensitive, long-fingered hand that had once held delicate surgical instruments and tackled the most intricate operations… until he'd somehow damaged it.

Simon dropped his hand at once, mistaking her glance for a warning look—*no touching*—until she looked up and let him see the glistening compassion in her eyes.

"How did you injure your hand?" she asked softly. "Is it still…?"

"No, it's fine now," he assured her, and grimaced. "Self-inflicted, I'm afraid. A moment of pure cussed-ness. I lost it and punched a brick wall."

Her eyes snapped wide in shock. "*Lost* it? How? Why? You mean…you were drunk? You didn't know what you were doing?" Why else would he have done such a crazy, destructive thing? Simon, who'd never drunk heavily, who'd never done anything to jeopardize his finely honed surgical skills. It didn't make sense.

"Oh, I knew what I was doing all right." There was no self-pity in his voice, only irony and self-mockery. "But I didn't care at the time."

"You didn't care about your career?" She stared at him in disbelief.

"I didn't care about anything. I'd lost my daughter, I'd lost the will to work—hard as I was driving myself at the time—and then I lost you." He glanced round, as if remembering there were others within earshot who could understand English. She could see him retreating and sensed, with a dip in her spirits, that he was regretting the admissions he'd already made. "Now's not the time to go into all that," he muttered.

She nodded, swallowing. Was he intending to tell her more later, when they *were* alone? Or was he slipping back into his dark, unreadable shell, shutting her out again?

I didn't care about anything, he'd said. Did that mean he was still too hurt and heartbroken about Lily to care what happened to him? Or had he "lost it" and punched that brick wall because he was hurt and angry that his wife had run out on him? Angry enough to lash out in a blind, self-destructive rage?

She'd thought at the time, with her husband so cold and distant, that he would have been *relieved* to see the back of her, that he wouldn't even care. Knowing that he blamed her in his heart for Lily's accident, she'd felt miserably sure that her presence must be a constant reminder of the baby daughter he'd lost, and that he wouldn't miss her when she was gone.

And yet…here he was in Venice, seeking her out again. *Why?* Simply because they'd met again purely by chance and he was curious about her life since she'd left him? Or…was there still some spark left of the love, the bond they'd once shared, enough to make him want to find out if it could flare into life again? She felt a quiver, a yearning deep down in her bruised heart.

She had to keep the lines of communication open. She couldn't bear it if he froze her out again.

"What's this about you going sailing for a year?" she asked, assuming the lightest tone she could manage. "In a yacht, you mean? Not by yourself, surely?" She'd never known him to go sailing before, or even to be interested in boats.

It made her realize soberly how little she knew about the man she'd married. They'd both been such high-powered, single-minded workaholics, even after Lily had arrived, that they'd barely had time to talk about the things that had happened to them in the past, before they'd met. Simon's past in particular—other than the little he'd told her about his mother and his ambitious career path, and the fact that his father had walked out on his family—had always been a closed book.

"Hell, no." The shutters had lifted, she saw with relief. He seemed amused at the idea that he might have sailed solo around the world. Or maybe he was just relieved at the change of subject. "There were twenty of us—mostly crew, and a handful of passengers. It wasn't a yacht exactly, it was a three-masted barque. A special round-the-world voyage, stopping off at various islands and foreign ports along the way. I applied for the job of medic."

A brilliant brain surgeon, taking on the lowly job of medic for a year... She searched his face, amazed there was no bitterness in his voice. He seemed resigned, rather than angry or upset.

Aware of her scrutiny, he gave a rough jerk of his shoulder. "I needed to get away. I needed time to think. To heal, I guess."

To heal? She gulped. Was he talking about his damaged hand? Or his heart, his soul? The heart she'd broken when she hadn't been able to react quickly enough on that pedestrian crossing and had failed to save Lily's pram from the erratic path of that speeding, out-of-control car.

"And...did it help?" she asked tentatively, half expecting to see him withdrawing again, his eyes turning bleak and remote again.

"By the end of the year's voyage, I felt I was ready to rejoin the human race...yeah," he said with his slow, crooked smile—the irresistible smile she'd fallen in love with on the first day they'd met, though she hadn't recognized it as love back then. "And to come looking for you," he added softly.

She stared at him, shakily aware of the sharp intensity of his blue eyes—no hint of remoteness there now. "You—you *knew* I was here in Venice?" Her head whirled. Their meeting in St. Mark's Square yesterday had been no accident? If true, at least it would explain why they'd bumped into each other here in Venice, of all the places in the world they could have chosen to visit. It had seemed such an amazing coincidence that they should both be here at the same time, in the first week of June. "How did you know?" she whispered.

"I called your London office and your secretary told me. No other details," he was quick to assure her, "except that you'd come here to recuperate after a bout of pneumonia." He raked a tanned hand through his dark hair, drawing her gaze upward for a mesmerized second. "How the hell did you come down with pneumonia?" he demanded. "I never knew you to have a cold in your life."

It was hard to tell if he cared or was being critical, blaming her again…for carelessness of a different sort. She gave a shrug. "I guess I was a bit run-down…with London's cold winter and taking on extra work and…and everything." He would know what *everything* meant.

"A lazy day on the beach at the Lido sounds like just the thing you need," he said out of the blue, surprising her with a tantalizing image of two sunbathing bodies lying side by side on soft warm sand—or, failing soft warm sand, on comfy sun lounges—revelling in the sun's healing warmth. Assuming he wanted to spend the day with her.

"If the weather stays like this, I might just do that," she murmured, trying not to show too much enthusiasm for the idea in case he didn't want to be a part of it.

Simon, noting that she'd said *I*, not *we*, decided not to push his luck. Let her get used to having him around again before trying to get too close and personal. He'd pushed too far yesterday and look at what had happened. He'd ended up brawling with her and jumping to all the wrong conclusions.

But damn it, she hadn't denied…

"How could you let me think you'd had another baby?" The bitter question leapt out.

He saw color flare in her cheeks. When she answered, he had to strain to catch what she said, her voice little more than a hoarse whisper.

"It was the way you just assumed…" She trailed off, then gave an impatient shake of her head. "When you lashed out at me I—I thought it was pointless going on talking to you, even trying to find common ground. You—you didn't seem to have changed…"

That hurt. She was still holding it against him? Still feeling he'd let her down?

"But you have changed," she conceded in a softer tone. "We—we've both changed."

"Yes." He glanced round. Much as he wanted to ask her about her life over the past two years—and knowing she must be equally curious about his wrecked career and what he intended to do in the future—a pressing queue in the busiest piazza in Venice was no place for those kind of confidences. They needed to be alone.

If she would agree to have lunch with him…a quiet, intimate lunch for two, maybe in one of the quieter, less crowded squares or alleys…

"That tour guide's actually quite informative," he remarked as the strident voice grew closer again. "If we listen in, we might find out what we missed seeing last time."

"Good idea," Annabel agreed, turning away from him to pay more attention to the woman's tireless spiel.

No more was said about spending a day at the Lido's famous beach resort or about their time apart. Before too long, the great doors of the Basilica were opened and they and the rest of the queue began to surge forward.

It was worth the wait. Just like four years ago, they found their senses assailed by the magnificence all around them—the dazzling gold mosaics; the exquisite *Pala d'Oro,* the famous gold, enamel and jewel-en-

crusted altarpiece; and the Galleria and Museum upstairs, home of the original gilded bronze horses. From
there, they had wonderful views of the Basilica's cav-
ernous interior and the awesome mosaics decorating the
huge central dome.

An hour passed, stretching into another. It was
only when he saw Annabel lean against a pillar that
Simon realized how tired she must be, and remembered that she was still recuperating from an energy-
sapping illness.

"Let's find a quiet place to sit down and grab a bite
to eat," he said, half expecting her to knock back the
offer and insist on going back to her hotel to rest. There
was still a wariness about her that sounded a warning.
*Don't push it. You've only just found her again and
she's plainly still upset that your so-called godlike surgical skills failed to save our baby daughter.* His heart
constricted at the agonizing memory.

It wasn't going to be easy. Far from it. In her eyes,
their marriage was dead, and it was going to take a
miracle to change her mind. She'd never wanted to settle down and get married in the first place. Marriage
had been forced on her. *He'd* forced it on her. And now
their reason for getting married had tragically gone,
leaving her free to concentrate on her soaring legal career, the career she'd worked so hard for and which
had always meant more to her than anything else in
her life.

"You know of a place?" she asked, and he felt some
of the heaviness lift from the black place deep inside
him. She hadn't run away *yet.* Maybe she was just curious about what he intended to do now that he was back.

in circulation, or maybe—hopefully—she felt a bit more than that, *wanted* a bit more than that.

At least she was giving him the chance to find out. And a chance, with luck, to mend some bridges and begin to heal the rift between them. *Could* she forgive him? Would she ever stop secretly blaming him? He'd blamed *her* for a black moment when he'd first heard about the accident, but that had changed once he'd learned the true circumstances. Maybe she could change, too, and learn to forgive *him*.

He sought her lovely green eyes and nodded. "Well, yes, I do, but we'll need to take a *vaporetto* ride along the Grand Canal to the Accademia Bridge. The concierge at the hotel recommended a place."

"Okay." She didn't even hesitate. "Lead the way."

The cooling breeze brushed Annabel's face as she stood beside Simon on the crowded deck of the slow, grinding water bus, watching the passing boats and elegant mansions along the Grand Canal and the shimmering reflections in the dancing green water. As a gondola carrying a young starry-eyed couple holding hands passed below them, it was suddenly rocked in the wash of the *vaporetto* and she felt memories of four years ago flood back. She flicked a glance at Simon.

Her eyes clashed with his, and she knew he was thinking of that day, too, remembering how she'd tumbled out of her rocking gondola into the Grand Canal and how he'd jumped in to rescue her. Would they ever recapture the magic of that exciting first meeting in Venice, and the blissful days that had followed?

What better place than magical Venice to recapture it!

* * *

"Well? Reckon this will do?"

"It's perfect." It was away from the crowds of tourists, in a spacious yet quiet square, with an old church, an imposing central statue, antique and fashion shops, and outdoor restaurants. Ristorante Masaniello was small and the staff friendly. A favorite of Venetians, the restaurant was famous for its fresh fish. The concierge had told them not to order off the tourist menu, and they didn't regret leaving it up to the expert staff to select their meal. Over one of the best lunches they'd ever enjoyed—a special Sicilian fish dish that was steamed and served with mint—it was Simon who asked the first question of the many that still hovered between them.

"Tell me how your job's going, Annabel."

She pursed her lips. The question he was really asking was: *Are you a partner yet?* "They made me an associate a year ago, but remember, this is an old, conservative law firm that still seems to prefer males as partners. Other top firms these days are more enlightened."

"You've never thought of jumping ship to a rival firm?" Simon asked. "I'm sure you'd have no trouble finding one that'd be keen to snap you up."

"You mean, give up and *leave?* No!" She was shocked. "It would be admitting defeat, and it wouldn't be loyal to Mallaby's. Besides, it's a very prestigious law firm and being a partner there would mean a lot to me and to my career. I'm determined to persevere and be their first female partner. If only to prove to myself that it's possible."

"Is that the only reason?" There was a knowing glint in his eye. "Only to yourself?"

She looked at him and twitched her lip. "Well, okay, maybe also to prove to my father that I can succeed in a male-dominated career and compete with the top guys. To prove to him and my brothers that women have an equally important role in the workplace, and don't just belong in the bedroom and kitchen."

"Your father still hasn't accepted it? Having a daughter who's chosen a high-powered career rather than the traditional housewife-and-mother role?"

She didn't answer for a second, wondering for the first time if he had some regrets himself that she hadn't become a full-time mother to Lily and a stay-at-home wife to him. But she quickly dismissed the notion. Simon had always been totally supportive and encouraging, never criticizing her long hours and agreeing without demur when she'd engaged a nanny to help take care of Lily while she was at work.

They'd been two of a kind...both equally driven, equally determined to reach their grand, high-flying goals. And what a price they'd paid. She shivered, trying to brush off the shadows.

"No. My father will never change," she said finally, hoping Simon would put her silence down to a daughter's pain at her father's inflexible, sexist attitude, not to regrets over their own lives. "Men like him never do. My brothers are just the same. They're both looking for wives like our mother—women willing to devote their lives to their husbands and children, with no independence or financial control for themselves."

The men in her family were the reason she'd left Queensland and fled south to Sydney to study law. To escape the stifling influence back home. Her father and two brothers ran a thriving family business, a forklift rental and sales business, Joe Hansen and Sons. And *Sons,* she reflected sourly. Only sons had any worth in the Hansen men's eyes.

"Maybe your mother's happy being a full-time wife and homemaker," Simon murmured.

"Happy!" She stabbed her fish with her fork. "She'd never admit it if she wasn't. She keeps up appearances, pretends her life and marriage are perfect, and turns a blind eye to my father's furtive little flings. Dad's careful never to go too far. He would never risk his marriage by flaunting his women. He has the life he wants and I guess he does care for my mother in his own selfish way. But she's trapped."

"Trapped? In this day and age?"

"Dad controls the finances. He keeps her comfortable enough not to rebel and he treats her okay…as long as she toes the line and keeps up the standards. She's little more than a pampered slave."

"I'm sure she'd find a way to leave if she really wanted to," Simon soothed, lifting his glass of wine and taking a long sip.

"She *doesn't* want to, and that's what I can't understand. I think she enjoys being a martyr, the so-called ideal wife and mother. She'd never break up the family, never disgrace her sons or her husband. The men in my family have her just where they want her."

"Not all men are like your father and brothers."

"No," she agreed, and flicked him a softer look. Simon was nothing like her father or brothers. She and Simon had been equals, neither wanting to outdo or make unreasonable demands on the other. And yet…

Her eyes wavered. He'd imposed his will on her in a different way, after Lily died. Closing up, shutting her out, hardly able even to look at her, except in the dark confines of their bed when he made love to her. *Or rather, had sex with her.* She stuffed a forkful of fish into her mouth.

"Did you see your parents before you left for London?" Simon asked, thinking she was brooding over them, not him.

"No, I just let them know I'd been transferred there from Sydney." She hadn't seen her family since they'd flown down from Brisbane for Lily's funeral.

That traumatic day…

She shivered. Her mother had been no comfort to her, too devastated at losing the baby granddaughter she'd rarely seen to think of anyone but herself and her own tragic loss. And her father had been his usual insensitive, chauvinistic self, growling, "I told you it's a mistake for a woman to have a full-time career and a family. Your mind must have been elsewhere when you crossed that road. Even on a pedestrian crossing, on a Sunday, you need to have your wits about you."

Because of her own feelings of guilt and black despair at the time, she hadn't flared back at him as she might have in the past. She'd even wondered if he could be right after all…that a woman couldn't expect to have both a career and a family without suffering dire consequences. She hadn't been able to face her parents since then, especially after she ran out on Simon and her marriage. She knew she couldn't expect any sympathy from them. Her father would see it as another failure, blaming her career, as always. And her mother would take his side, as usual.

"Why are we talking about my parents?" she grumbled. "You know it always upsets me. I came to Venice to feel better, not worse."

"And I'm going to make sure you do feel better," Simon said without missing a beat. "Assuming you want me to stick around?"

I'll always want you around, Simon...as long as you don't shut me out again...as long as you can bring yourself to talk about what happened two years ago and stop silently blaming me, or, at least try to be more understanding and sympathetic.

She raised her glass in a brave salute, wondering if it was already too late to pick up the pieces. He still hadn't opened up to her...about the things that really mattered. The loss of their daughter...the loss of his career, though that, she hoped, was only temporary...and the cold, hard fact that they both lived on opposite sides of the world now, she in London, he in Sydney. Now that he'd had his healing year off, his old hospital must be clamouring to have him back.

The hospital where Lily died...

Her hand trembled on her wine glass. Simon had tried so hard to save his daughter, but he must have known in his heart, as all the doctors around him had known, that she was beyond saving. He'd had to watch his baby girl slip away beneath his fingers, the expert fingers that were trying so desperately to save her life. With that heartrending memory to haunt him, how could he ever face going back there?

But there were plenty of other Australian hospitals that must be aware of Simon's outstanding skills and reputation, many surely eager to grab him if they had the chance.

* * *

Simon lifted his own glass and clinked it against hers. She hadn't answered his question, he noted, but she hadn't given him the boot, either. Not *yet*.

"To recovery," he said. She could take that whichever way she liked. The recovery of her health…the recovery of trust after their horrendous loss…the recovery of their shattered marriage…even, thinking positively, the recovery of romance in their lives.

What better place to rediscover romance than here in romantic Venice, where they'd first found it? Maybe he should think no further than that…romancing her, wooing her all over again, rediscovering the passion they'd lost. Maybe even embarking on a romantic second honeymoon, to revive the old magic, the old chemistry, before they had to leave Venice and face reality again.

He looked deep into the shadowed green of her eyes. Two people in love, damn it, could face anything, overcome any obstacle. They'd managed to do it once before, hadn't they? As compulsive workaholics with a shared ambition to reach the top of their respective fields and with no thought of marriage or settling down, they'd had to face the fact that they were going to have a baby together.

Yeah…even though they'd allowed their work, rather than their relationship, to consume them, they'd made their marriage work once, for a while, at least. Until the loss of…he felt his throat catch. Until the worst tragedy of their lives had torn them apart.

It'll be different this time, he vowed, burying the old pain and letting his eyes caress hers as his senses drank in the subtle, familiar fragrance of her. They just needed to change a few things, make more time for each other, avoid the same mistakes, and to talk more, open up more, face their ghosts, something he'd always found difficult.

Damn it, he still did.

Annabel felt a jolt, like an electric charge, zip through her. Something had just changed…something in him…in his eyes, in the way the veiled blue suddenly cleared…in the way he was looking at her.

It was the way he'd looked at her four years ago, when they first met…as if he were seeing her for the first time, and was excited by what he saw. She remembered the way she'd responded back then…and could feel herself responding in a similar way now. It felt…it felt as if they'd gone back in time and were starting all over again.

Was it possible, after the harsh words they'd flung at each other yesterday, and the bitter, painful memories of their last months together?

But that's just it, you fool. He wants you to forget all that for now, to forget all the bad things, the pain, the hurt, and grab this chance to start again…from scratch.

She felt her heart lift, and looked up, flashing a sudden dazzling smile. "We're wasting time just sitting here. There's a lot we've yet to explore in Venice. Ready to go?"

"Let me just pay the bill."

"No, let me pay for *you*. Please."

He didn't argue. They'd always shared costs in the past. Something her father would never have abided in a woman, she mused as she pulled out her purse.

They walked back across the Accademia Bridge and decided, since it was open, to visit the Accademia Gallery. As expected, they found it an absolute treasure-house of magnificent Venetian paintings.

They spent the rest of the afternoon wandering down narrow alleys with flower boxes overflowing with orange and pink geraniums and washing drying overhead, following small winding canals and crossing narrow bridges, discovering other treasures they'd missed four years ago, like the great Franciscan church known as the Frari, where they gazed in awe at the famous Titian and Bellini masterpieces.

Returning to the nearest *vaporetto* station, Annabel bought a few postcards to send back to her colleagues at work, and one to send back home to Brisbane, just to let her parents know she was still alive. *Having a short holiday in Venice, you should both come here sometime.* No need to mention Simon, or that she'd been ill. Let them think her new life as an unattached career woman was perfect.

Back at St. Mark's Square, after a return *vaporetto* ride down the Grand Canal, they joined a short queue outside the towering *Campanile* and caught the lift up to the top of the bell tower for spectacular views of sun-drenched Venice and the Lagoon.

"What a sight," she breathed, darting from one side to the other. "Now I know what they mean by a bird's eye-view. You can see everything!"

"Not quite everything. Haven't you noticed something is missing from up here?" Simon was standing so close behind her she could feel his breath spreading the fine hairs on her head.

"What?" she asked, her voice husky. Right now all she could think of was him and how tempted she felt to turn around and…

Cool it, you idiot. A crowded bell tower's hardly the place for romantic canoodling.

Simon's voice rumbled back. "You can see the whole of Venice lying below, but you can't see any canals. Not even the Grand Canal, except where it runs into the Lagoon."

She stared downward. "Good heavens, you're right, you can't. Not a single one. How amazing." Almost as amazing as it was to be back here in Venice, alone with her estranged husband. If you could call being among crowds of tourists alone.

"Time we were going down," Simon said, glancing at his watch. "Let's go."

"What's the hurry?" she asked as he ushered her back to the lift. Did he have to meet someone? Tom, maybe?

He grinned. "The bells strike on the hour, and we don't want to be deafened."

"Oh." She glanced up at the five huge bells and felt a twinge of relief that he wasn't leaving her for someone else.

"Want to head back to the hotel now for a rest?" he asked when they and a dozen or so others spilled out of the crowded lift.

The prospect of putting her feet up for a while made her realize how footsore and weary she was after all the walking they'd done. Her bout of pneumonia had hit her hard and she still tired easily.

"Okay," she said, glancing up at Simon, wondering if she looked as worn out as she felt.

"You must be tired...not that you look it," he was quick to assure her, as if he'd read her thoughts. It was something he hadn't done for a long time, it struck her—bothered to read her mind, or care what she was thinking. "The sunshine and exercise are obviously doing you the world of good," he said. "You've a healthy glow in your cheeks that wasn't there yesterday."

She flushed, suspecting it wasn't just the sunshine and exercise that were making her glow. "My legs are tired," she admitted, just as bells started chiming in the tower, "and my feet *are* a bit sore. I can't remember when I've done so much walking. But it's been fun," she said, and meant it.

"It's probably just what you've been needing."

Or maybe I've just been needing you, Simon.

Simon squared his shoulders as the dusky rose-colored walls of their hotel appeared. Much as he was determined to be patient and not rush her, he couldn't resist leading her a little further.

"Want to meet me in the dining room for a spot of dinner later?" he asked. "Or we could find a restaurant nearby if you'd prefer. Your friends have their conference dinner tonight, so we're not likely to run into them." He wondered if she was as relieved as he was at the thought. His hands clenched as he saw her hesitate.

"I...actually, I've offered to mind their baby daughter Gracie tonight, while they're at their dinner. I left a note for Tessa this morning. If she leaves a bottle for the baby, she can enjoy herself without worrying about feeds."

Her tone was faintly defensive and he shot her a speculative look. Was it because she was talking about a baby? Because she was still sore at him for lashing out at her yesterday after seeing her with Tessa's baby and assuming it was hers?

Or was she challenging him to think of their own baby, he wondered heavily, and to face up to the fact that he hadn't been able to save her? Hell, as if he *hadn't* faced up to·it! He'd been living with the guilt and despair for the past two years! Damn it, he'd been living with guilt and regret all his life. His father had made sure of that.

He ran a frustrated hand through his hair. If his wife still hadn't forgiven him, if being with him again hadn't softened her at all, what hope did he have?

A distant, unbearable memory—one he'd long suppressed, unable to face the shameful, gut-wrenching reality—stirred in the depths of his psyche. An image of a small white face with snowy-blond hair appeared. He snapped it from his mind, a silent groan rolling through him. If she knew about *that,* knew how he'd failed someone *else* close to him, what hope would he ever have of winning her back?

Would he be mad to even try?

Annabel noted the change in him and turned away with a sigh. He couldn't even talk about *Tessa's* baby. She pushed through the doors of the hotel before he could open them for her.

"I'll just check my mail." She was already veering away from him, heading for the reception desk. "Thanks for…a nice day." It sounded lame, but she wasn't ready to admit how much she'd enjoyed being with him.

She heard his voice curling after her. "You'll still need to eat tonight. Join me if you can."

With the baby, he meant. He just couldn't say the word *baby*. She bit down hard on her lip. She'd suffered the same difficulty herself over the past two years…. until the warmth of little Gracie snuggling into her yesterday had seeped into the cold space that Lily had left inside her, filling her with a warmth she'd thought she would never feel again.

When she gave her room number to the man at the desk, he handed her a note. It was from Tessa.

You're an angel, Annabel, but we're okay, thanks, the conference committee have arranged a babysitter. So good of you to offer. Catch up soon. Tessa.

Gracie already had a babysitter. She felt a twinge of regret, mingled with something else—a zing of expectancy, a buzz of excitement. Now she could meet Simon for dinner…if she wished. Alone, just the two of them.

Did she really want to? Or was she allowing herself to get too caught up, too soon? What had really changed? The accident to Simon's hand had certainly changed his working life, forcing him to slow down, posing new challenges to him, but had *he* changed?

Chapter Four

Annabel felt well refreshed after a rest and a hot shower. She hesitated over a black cocktail dress before pulling on a skirt and scoop-necked olive top, not wanting to dress up for dinner when it was just an ad hoc arrangement with Simon. *Join me if you can.*

When she walked into the dining room at seven-thirty, there was no sign of him. She was surprised at the stab of disappointment she felt. Of course, he'd be expecting her to have baby Gracie with her—if he turned up at all. Had he decided he didn't want to have dinner with a baby in tow? Or did he think she'd be having a meal in her room?

"Buona sera, signora." Josef, the head waiter, greeted her with his usual welcoming smile. He led her to a secluded corner table. It was set for two, but she knew that didn't mean anything—there were always tables set ready for guests who wanted to dine in.

She ordered a mineral water and as she sipped it, she perused the menu without much enthusiasm. She'd hoped she wouldn't be dining alone, something she'd done far too much of in the past two years—usually in the privacy of her rented apartment back in London.

Just as she made up her mind to order a main course and then make her escape, Simon appeared, breezing in from the direction of the foyer.

She felt a smile burst from her lips.

The sight of that warm smile sent a ripple of relief through Simon, unravelling the knot that had coiled in his gut. When she'd left him this afternoon she'd looked as if she couldn't get away from him fast enough. Would she be smiling like that if she didn't want to see him again?

"I was having a drink at the bar," he said, bending down to kiss her on the cheek, though he longed to sweep her into his arms and plunder her soft lips, and every other part of her as well. "I asked Josef to signal to me when you arrived." His gaze flicked round. "Where's…?"

"Gracie?" She looked up at him, searching his eyes for a disconcerting moment. Not hard to guess why, he thought ruefully. He hadn't reacted well to babies so far. And who could blame him? A day ago, he'd thought his wife had had another man's baby. And for the past two years he'd been trying to deal with the death of his *own* baby. *Their* baby.

"Tessa already had a babysitter," she said, letting her eyelashes sweep down again, hiding whatever was in those expressive green eyes. "I was just about to order."

"You go ahead," he said, focussing his mind on dinner. Dinner with his wife. "I'll have what you're having." He waved away a menu as Josef approached the table. "Annabel's going to order for both of us."

She looked suddenly flustered, and he wondered if she was remembering how they'd sometimes ordered for each other when they were first married, when one arrived late for a rare dinner together after work. They'd always been in a hurry in those days, never wanting to waste time because their working days were so full and their hours so long—and their free evenings so short. They'd had even less time after...

He gritted his teeth. It was still hard to think of their baby daughter and the tragically short, precious time they'd had her. And worse, the scant time they'd given her when they'd had the chance.

They'd both steered clear of the painfully difficult subject since meeting up again yesterday, especially after he'd rashly accused her of having a new lover and a new baby and ended up with egg all over his face.

But he knew they were going to have to talk about their heartrending loss before anything could be resolved between them. He felt his palms moisten. Damn it! Why did the very thought always make him break out in a cold sweat?

Get a grip, Pacino. They'd only just met up again. Before dealing with the deep, difficult stuff, they needed to get closer and feel more comfortable with each other, needed to find out if the old magic was still there...if *anything* was still there.

It *is* there...

He'd felt it simmering between them all day, the sexual tension, the prickling excitement, the electric awareness. Yeah…she still felt something, and that was the place to start. The one place where there'd never been a problem.

He felt Annabel's eyes on him and gave her a reassuring smile, letting his eyes caress hers for a brief moment, wondering if she'd been reading his thoughts… and if she shared them.

Her voice, when she spoke, had a slight tremor. "I was only going to have a main course. The veal escalope with vegetables. Um…but won't you want an appetizer first, Simon? The risotto, maybe?"

"One course'll suit me, too," he said, and nodded to Josef. "The veal for both of us, *per favore*. And I'll have a whiskey while we're waiting…*grazie.*" When Josef had moved away he turned back to Annabel. "If we don't linger too long over dinner, we'll have a chance to watch the sun setting. They say there's a magnificent view from the rooftop garden."

He saw a tinge of pink seep into her cheeks. "Is there?" Her eyes lifted to his, limpid green in the soft light. "I'd love to see it."

He felt his smile widen…a warmly satisfied smile.

Annabel attacked her meal with more gusto than she'd expected to feel when she'd first arrived. Simon had seemed a bit distracted earlier and she'd been afraid he was withdrawing again, closing her out again, but he'd relaxed since then and been a perfect dinner companion, really turning on the charm. He'd always had charm and charisma in the past—in the days when they'd been happy—but his charm had died along with Lily. Now it was back in force.

It felt almost like it had four years ago when they first met…two people attracted to each other, excited to be together, yet not too sure about each other just yet… both acutely aware of each other, eager to please, giving their full attention to each other, while steering clear of anything too delicate or personal.

More alive than she'd felt for a couple of years, she found herself reeling under his spell, as she'd reeled under it back then.

"Want any dessert?" he asked as their empty plates were whisked away. "You have a choice of their home-made cakes. We might just have time."

"Let's not risk it," she said, feeling her heart pick up a beat. "We don't want to miss that sunset."

They took the lift up to the rooftop, a large tiled area with groups of chairs and covered tables, shaded swinging lounges and terra-cotta pot plants, and marvellous views over the glassy Lagoon and the array of boats below. Beyond they could see the Grand Canal and the domed rooftops and spires of Venice.

"Wow. Just look," she whispered in awe. The sky was aglow with pink and gold as a vermilion sun sank over a city that seemed to be floating on liquid gold.

"Magnificent," Simon breathed from close behind, and she felt the warmth of his hands curl over her shoulders. She felt an overwhelming urge to lean back into him, but she fought it for a wary second…just a second, before giving in to the urge and melting against him. She'd missed him so much, missed the comfort of his hard, sexy body close to hers, missed the sensual thrill of being in his arms…the only man she'd ever wanted, ever needed…ever loved.

His arms wrapped round her from behind, cradling her close, letting her feel his body's warmth as he pressed his lips into her hair.

"I've missed you, Bel," he murmured, using the name he hadn't uttered since...since... She felt herself tensing, remembering the way he'd changed since the trauma of losing Lily, the way he'd turned away from her at a time when she'd needed him the most. It would be so easy to give in, to take what he was offering, to give him what she longed with all her heart to give, but what would it solve? They'd still had sex after Lily had died but it hadn't brought them any closer, hadn't made him open up to her, hadn't drawn any comforting words from him, or murmurs of forgiveness, or exposed what was in his heart.

If she gave in now, it would be like before. He'd feel he could have her, make love to her, without having to share his secret thoughts and feelings, thinking that his virile body, his potent physical loving, would be enough.

As she stirred in his arms, a small bird-like woman, followed by a portly, silver-haired man, clattered out onto the rooftop.

"My, would you look at that sunset, honey!" The woman darted forward to get a better view. An American, with a broad Southern accent. "You never see sunsets like this back home." Entranced as she was, curiosity got the better of her and she wrenched her gaze away from the view. "Honeymooners?" she asked, eyeing Simon and Annabel with a knowing gleam in her eye.

When Simon just smiled and made no move to break his embrace, Annabel had the alarmed feeling he was prepared to go along with the false notion and she stammered a quick, "Just—just friends." She had no intention of adding to the complications they already had in their lives. Next, this woman would be telling the entire hotel staff they were on their honeymoon, and then Tessa and Tom would hear, and everyone would start wondering what was going on and why they had separate rooms, and…oh heck, where would it all end?

She wriggled out of his clasp, and felt relief, and a faint chill when he stepped back, his arms sliding away.

"*Good* friends," Simon drawled, and she heard the amused note in his voice. She sensed that if she turned and looked into his eyes she'd see an equally roguish gleam in the blue depths…just like the Simon of old.

He's enjoying this, she thought unsteadily. *Just because I had a moment of weakness, he thinks I'm ready to fall back into his arms, no questions asked. Well, it's not going to be that easy….*

The American woman beamed, satisfied with Simon's answer. "Ambrose and I had our honeymoon here forty years back and here we are again for our fortieth wedding anniversary. Maybe you'll come back for yours. Venice is the most romantic place on Earth." She gave a conspiratorial wink. "Sorry we butted in on your private moment."

"No, no, you didn't, we were just going," Annabel babbled, already swinging away. "We'll leave you to enjoy the view in peace. Coming, Simon?"

"Yes, darling."

Darling! When had he last called her *darling?* A long time ago, and certainly never with that mocking undertone.

Oh, yes, he was enjoying this. Well, she wasn't ready

for his slick endearments, even if he was only doing it to tease the American couple. If she gave him the slightest encouragement, he'd be calling her *darling* all the time, using that same bantering tone, and she'd never know if he meant it or not.

"I'm going back to my room," she said, diving down the stairs and beetling along the passage to the lift. She badly needed some breathing space. "I've some washing to do and postcards to write."

"Good idea," Simon said without demur. "You've had a long day."

"Yeah." She pressed the button impatiently until the lift came. "You going up, too?" she asked as the doors opened. "Or are you going out?" For a brief second, she felt tempted to join him if he was, to make the most of her short time here in Venice, but she curbed the urge. She needed that breathing space. Maybe he did, too.

"I might just have a nightcap down at the bar," he said. He didn't ask her to join him. "Want to go to the Lido tomorrow?" he asked as she stepped into the lift. He held the door open, waiting for her answer. "We could hire bikes and explore the island, then go and laze on the beach when the day warms up."

Hire *bikes?* She paused, bemused at this new Simon she was seeing. She'd never seen him ride a bike once during their marriage, and she hadn't ridden a bike since her school days. It sounded fun. They hadn't allowed themselves time for much fun together during their marriage. They'd always been working. Working or taking care of Lily. *Not enough care...*

She blinked the painful thought away.

"Well, yes, if you like," she heard herself agreeing.

She'd be back at work soon enough. Might as well enjoy all the fresh air and exercise she could get.

"Good. See you at breakfast...or whenever you're ready." Simon let the door go and it slid across, shutting him from her sight.

She leaned against the lift wall and inhaled a deep breath, letting it out in a whistling sigh. Another day gone and they were still talking, if guardedly, still wanting to see more of each other. In fact, tonight they'd done more than just talk. They'd actually made physical contact.

Physical contact... She gave a scoffing snort. How cold and clinical that sounded. Fleeting as the contact had been, it certainly hadn't been cold *or* clinical.

Far from it.

When Simon appeared at breakfast the next morning, he saw Tom and Tessa already settled at a table in the inner room. He was tempted to simply wave and leave them to it, but Tom beckoned him over. They had their baby with them and this time the child was wide awake, gurgling in her capsule. She reminded him so strongly of his own baby daughter that the old raw, primitive grief welled in his throat, threatening to choke off his breath.

"Come and join us, Simon. We're flying home today. Home being Chicago these days," he reminded them, "not Melbourne." There was a cocky note in Tom's voice, as if he considered Chicago a few notches above his old home town Down Under. He waved to a vacant chair. "Sit down, mate."

Simon held up a hand. "You two go ahead... I'll

find another table and wait for Annabel." Even if she didn't come down, it would be a relief to be away from Tom, avoiding a possible grilling.

It came anyway.

"Will you be going back to Sydney?" Tom asked before he could back away. "You don't want to be away from surgery for too long, mate…if you're thinking of going back to it."

Simon had had too much practice at hiding his feelings to show them now to a man he cared little about. He waved a careless hand. No one looking at him would have guessed at the darkness clawing at his gut. "I've some commitments here in Europe to deal with before I go back to Australia," he said with an air of finality. With a quick smile for Tessa and a trite, "Good to catch up," for Tom, he swung away before Tom could quiz him further.

He stepped over to the breakfast buffet to help himself to croissants and coffee, whisking them to a vacant table in the open garden courtyard, safely away from Tom and Tessa, hoping that Annabel would join him there, and soon.

When she appeared it was like a lightbulb bursting inside him, chasing away the darkness that had coiled in his gut and warming the cold recesses of his battered heart. Seeing her slight figure in a simple white top and ankle-length pants, following the familiar sway of her hips and drinking in her luminous green eyes and soft enticing lips, he knew that here was the only thing in the world, the only *person* in the world, who was capable of healing the scars in his heart and making him whole again…if that were still possible. No amount of solitude, or mental purgatory, or roaming on the high seas had been able to do it. Only Annabel could give his life meaning.

But did she want to?

And even if she did, what could he give to her. What did she want from him? Did she *want* to mend the shattered fragments of their lives and salvage their marriage?

Annabel felt Simon's eyes on her as she walked into the breakfast room, where the attractive garden courtyard was opened to the morning sun.

Something in his eyes as he rose to greet her jolted her, locking her gaze to his. As she came closer, she could see a swirl of emotion in his eyes, emotions he'd hidden from her for far too long and that snagged the breath in her throat to see now, even though she couldn't read them. She barely had a chance to as his tanned face creased in a broad smile equally devastating to her senses, a smile that scrunched up those glittering blue eyes and hid all those whirling emotions, revealing only warm twinkles of pleasure.

"*Buongiorno,* Annabel," he said, his deep voice reverberating through her body. "Why don't you fetch some breakfast and join me? By the way, our friends Tom and Tessa are here...in the inner room, out of sight from here. They're going home today, Tom told me."

"Oh, are they?" She was surprised at the relief she felt. She liked Tessa, but it would be good not to have any distractions. She wanted Simon to herself. "I'd better pop over and say goodbye."

She moved away, quickly finding them in their secluded corner. As she greeted Tessa and Tom she saw baby Gracie at their feet, wide awake in her carry-cot, and felt her heart give its usual flutter. But rather than wanting to run, to resist close contact, she bent down to smile at the baby and brush the child's smooth rosy cheek with a tender finger, feeling her senses assailed by the baby's sweet, familiar scent. Though her heart ached from her own loss, she felt a fuzzy warmth flow through her at the intimate connection—which must, she thought hopefully, be a positive step in the healing process.

"I've just come to say goodbye. I hear you're leaving today. It's been lovely to meet you, it really has." The words came out in a rush. She was hoping they'd simply return the sentiments and let her go, but it was too much to hope for.

"Are you and Simon going to hitch up together?" Tessa blurted out. "We think you're both so perfect for each other."

She felt her senses spin. "I…we…" For a second she couldn't form a coherent answer. How would Tessa know, from a single meeting, that she and Simon were perfect for each other? Tessa knew nothing about them. She had no idea.

She considered simply laughing and moving away, but she knew Tessa was only being kind and wanted her to be as happy as she and Tom. She pulled herself together and tried again, putting a smile in her voice. "Look, we've only just met up again after…after quite a while. I don't know what's going to happen. How did your dinner dance go last night? I bet you were the belle of the ball, Tessa."

Tessa was happy to take the hint, her eyes shining as she turned to Tom, letting him answer for her.

"I had to watch her all night or I could easily have lost her," he said with smooth gallantry, taking her hand and kissing it, showing, Annabel thought, that he genuinely cared about his wife and didn't only think of himself. "I've never seen her looking lovelier."

"I'm glad you had a good night," she said warmly. She had her equilibrium back, the steadiness back in her voice. "I'd better go and get some breakfast. Have a good trip back, won't you? Hope we meet up again some day."

Some day... She felt a catch in her step as she made for the breakfast table with Tessa's "Best of luck, Annabel," echoing after her. She wondered how she would feel if they did meet up again in a few years time. Little Gracie would be older, a toddler by then, or a schoolgirl.

Lily would never grow older, never go to school, never meet a boy or become a radiant bride... or become Australia's first woman prime minister, as she and Simon had once half-jokingly proposed.

She squeezed her eyes shut as she bent over the selection of cereals on offer. She couldn't go back to Simon with those kinds of thoughts in her mind. He might sense it and withdraw from her again. They'd never been able to offer consolation to each other, never been able to talk about their tragic loss. And yet...and yet...

She swallowed. If they were to have any hope for the future, they would have to talk about Lily. And *soon*.

By the time she rejoined Simon, she was in control

again. It was something she'd had a lot of practice at...
being in control. She would never have been able to
function properly in her high-powered law firm if she
hadn't been able to control her emotions. Until she'd
fallen sick, and at the height of her illness—or rather,
the depths—had fallen in a heap, luckily in the hospital, out of sight of her colleagues. But she wasn't going
to think about that bad time, either. She was here in Venice to get fit and strong again. To show the partners of
her firm, and herself, that she was up to the job.

More than just up to the job—that she was still
keenly ambitious and aiming for the top, for a coveted
partnership.

"You've made your farewells?" Simon asked as she
sat down and began sipping her orange juice. She knew
what he was really asking. *Did they quiz you about us?*

"Yep." She kept her eyes lowered and her voice calm.
"They were just telling me about their conference dinner last night, and what a triumph Tessa was in her new
evening gown." She knew she was chickening out, not
mentioning Tessa's loaded question, but she wasn't sure
she could laugh it off, and the alternative—discussing
it seriously—wasn't a topic for the breakfast table. And
anyway, it was too soon to face those kinds of decisions.

Besides, Tom and Tessa might take it into their heads
to come over for a final farewell when they'd finished
their breakfast, and she wouldn't want to be caught in the
midst of a deep and meaningful discussion with Simon.

"So...you still want to go to the Lido today?" she
asked, only now raising her eyes. If he saw any waver-
ing in them, let him put it down to the thought of spending the day together.

"Of course…if you do. Feeling up to that bike ride?"

Her competitive juices kicked in. "You think you could outride me? Assuming you can ride at all." She let her eyes challenge him.

"You'll have to find out, won't you?" His own eyes danced, lifting her spirits. If they could take the time to kid around, there was hope for them yet.

They hadn't spent enough time kidding around during their marriage. They'd both been too busy working, too driven, too determined to be the best in their respective fields, and they'd had a baby to think about as well. And just as Simon had reached the heights he'd been aiming for and she'd been close to her own goal, they'd lost Lily, and their lives had self-destructed…but she wasn't going to think about that now.

"We'd better get on with our breakfast," she said, attacking her cereal. "The sooner we leave, the sooner you can show me if you can ride a bike or not."

"That goes both ways. Remember, I've never seen you ride, either. Oh, and you'd better take your togs and a towel for the beach. If you intend to go for a swim." The teasing light was back in his eyes, enhancing the ravishing blue. "You probably think you can outswim me as well."

"I reckon I could give it a shot." When had they last swum together? In the hotel pool during their brief weekend honeymoon on the Gold Coast? She felt a dreamy nostalgia. You could hardly call that a proper swim. They'd just bobbed around, making eyes at each other and kissing a lot. And laughing a lot. Maybe today, at the Lido, they'd recapture some of that early carefree togetherness…if it were possible.

Chapter Five

It was only a short *vaporetto* ride across the Lagoon to the Lido, a long slender island with lush greenery and trees—something they'd rarely seen in Venice. A huge green-domed mausoleum and a hodgepodge of hotels, red-roofed buildings and multistory apartment buildings cluttered the shoreline. It was also surprising to see cars and buses driving along the streets.

Annabel felt a ripple of expectancy as she and Simon spilled out onto the landing stage with the other passengers. The thought of spending a day alone with her estranged husband at a popular beachside resort... A week ago, she would never have believed it.

She was acutely aware of her new floral bikini under her sleeveless white top and ankle-length pants. She'd bought it on a whim before leaving London, thinking it unlikely she'd have a chance to wear it. It was a long time since she'd revealed her body to Simon…or any man, for that matter. Would he find her too thin and pale now for his taste, and yearn for the old voluptuous curves?

Simon was feeling the same buzz of anticipation, wondering about the day ahead. He hoped it would be fun and remind her of happier, more carefree times together, make her realize they could be happy with each other again. He would do anything in his power—anything—to win back the love she'd withdrawn from him and make things right between them. Their lighthearted banter over breakfast had buoyed his spirits and given him hope.

"I'll just ask where we can hire bikes," he said, grabbing a likely looking local. He reeled off a question in fluent Italian, and the man nodded, gesticulating with both hands, gabbling a reply so fast that Annabel was sure she wouldn't have understood him even if she'd learned to speak Italian.

"Grazie, signor." Simon gave the man a beaming smile. "It's just across the road and around a bit." He grabbed Annabel's hand. "This way." All around them people were surging this way and that, heading north, south and inland.

"Popular place," she commented as he steered her across the road. "The summery weather's brought everyone out."

"The Lido's always crowded at this time of year. One of the hazards of…Hey, watch out!" He jerked her back against him. "There are cars here, don't forget."

"Yeah…I know. Don't they know there are pedestrians, too?" It seemed strange to see cars, buses and motor scooters again, to have to share roads with them after the traffic-free alleys and squares of Venice.

Ten minutes later, they had their bikes, Annabel's a regular-sized ladies' bike and Simon's a shiny red contraption that looked big even for him. They pulled them to the side of the road to mount. They'd both brought backpacks, leaving their hands free.

"We'll head south," said Simon, taking charge.

"Oh? You know your way around?" Peering at him through her sunglasses, Annabel adjusted the peaked cap she'd worn to shade her face.

"I did some homework last night."

So that's what he'd been doing after she left him. Not spending his night in the bar. "Right. South it is."

"Keep to the side of the road," Simon commanded as she took off with only the slightest wobble.

She felt a surge of elation, mixed with pure adrenaline. "Come on, what's keeping you?" she called out, glancing round with a grin—nearly losing her balance and careering into the ditch alongside.

"Coming. You just watch what you're doing. I'll stay behind you."

When she glanced round again he was a few feet behind, riding like a pro. He would, she thought ruefully, wishing she felt more confident herself. He'd always done well at everything she'd seen him do. Handling a car. Mending a fuse. Cooking a barbecue steak on a warm Sunday evening. Swimming. *Diving into canals to save people.* Sailing the world would be the same, she had no doubt. Like a duck to water.

Where did her own limited expertise lie? She'd

barely allowed herself enough spare time to read a novel or go to a movie.

Driven. She was far too driven.

She began to wobble again as a car sped past and decided she'd better concentrate and start taking in her surroundings, or this picturesque ride along the tree-lined streets of the Lido would be wasted.

It was a glorious day, growing warmer by the second, and the air was filled with other sounds she hadn't heard in Venice—the sound of birds cheeping and chirruping in the trees, the screech of brakes, the growl of a bus. Occasionally they passed other cyclists, and they smiled and waved to each other. It was all very pleasant. If only she and Simon had spent more time like this together—doing nothing but enjoying each other's company—instead of working all the time, and snatching time with their baby daughter when they could.

Maybe they would have…in time…if they'd had the chance. If their world hadn't collapsed, and their marriage with it.

But she mustn't think about any of that. Not today.

"Nice houses," she remarked, hoping they'd have a chance to talk about more personal, meaningful things as the day went on. Hoping he would finally unlock his closed heart and really talk to her.

"Yeah, the rich flock here in the summer months." Simon's deep voice rumbled after her. "A pleasant change to see trees and hedges and greenery again, too, after those bare stone alleys and canals of Venice, quaint as they are."

"And a relief to get away from all those tourists," she called back.

"Wait till we get to the beach." He meant the crowds, but it conjured up other pictures as well…more tantalizing pictures.

After a while, they stumbled across a small cemetery. It looked so exquisite, so beautifully tended, that they decided to stop for a closer look. It was the first time either of them had been able to face a cemetery since Lily's death. They'd laid their daughter to rest beside Simon's mother in Melbourne, but they'd never gone back there together, throwing themselves into their work to escape their pain and their demons.

An old woman was there putting flowers on a grave. She looked up and said something to Annabel that she couldn't understand, perhaps thinking they were looking for relatives in the cemetery. But it didn't seem to matter if they understood or not. A few nods and smiles, and they were friends. The old lady's warmth stayed with them as they rode on. Perhaps it was another step forward in the healing process, Annabel mused hopefully.

They passed through a small village and took time out to look at its charming old church and buy ice cream before heading towards the beaches.

They didn't speak again for a while, both lost in their own thoughts. Annabel felt emotion welling inside her, sensing they weren't alone, aware of a haunting presence here with them—*between* them. And the ghost of their beloved daughter would always come between them, threatening their relationship, she thought sadly, if they couldn't talk about her, share their loss, grieve together.

"I miss my little girl so much," she said pensively, and realized she'd spoken aloud.

"*Our* little girl," came a somber voice from close behind. "I miss her, too, Bel. I'll always miss her. I loved her, too."

Her heart jumped. There was no censure in his voice, just a sadness to match her own.

She looked at him, a tentative smile on her lips. No need to say more now…especially not with traffic whizzing past and their bikes to think about. They needed to concentrate.

She realized they were following a leafy road with a canal running alongside. Dinghies were moored along one side of the canal and narrow covered barges lined the other. A grassy verge, shaded by flickering, fairylike trees, lay between them and a sharp fall into the canal.

"Isn't it pretty?" she said, pulling up without warning to have a more leisurely look at the boats below and the trees reflected in the water. "Let's just—oh *heck!*" She'd forgotten that Simon was so close behind. To avoid her he slewed round, somehow losing control of his bike. She saw it crash, almost in slow motion, into the grass, throwing Simon down with it, miraculously avoiding the nearest tree.

For a shocked second, she thought he was going to roll into the canal, and had visions of having to jump in and rescue him the way he'd once rescued her. The thought made her giggle. When she saw him land safely in the grass a peal of hysterical laughter—part relief, part amusement—erupted from her throat.

"So…you think you can outride me, do you?" she taunted, the melancholy of a moment ago floating away. "Doesn't look like it. You can't even stay on your bike!"

She was laughing so much, she had tears in her eyes and didn't notice for a moment that he wasn't getting up. "Simon?" She blinked, looked closer, and frowned. Why wasn't he getting up? Why was he just lying there, his head tilted awkwardly to one side? Had he hit his head on a rock lying hidden in the grass?

She let her bike fall and leapt over to him, dropping to her knees beside him, an icy fear gripping her heart.

"Simon! Simon, what's wrong?" His eyes were closed, his well-built body ominously still. His deep tan made it hard to tell if his face was deathly pale underneath. She leaned over him to check if he was still breathing, sending up a silent prayer and hoping she'd be able to remember the CPR he'd once taught her.

She put her ear close to his mouth and couldn't detect any breath! She fought a wave of panic. *Think! Think!* She remembered to tilt back his head, forcing his lips apart. *The kiss of life first...*

She brought her open mouth down on his.

And felt strong arms clamp round her waist, felt herself being rolled onto her side in the grass.

At the same time, the mouth still attached to hers came suddenly alive, claiming her lips with his own in a way no unconscious man would be able to do. She gave a squeak of outrage, realizing he'd duped her. The rat! But much as she was tempted to shove him straight into the canal and leave him there, she didn't want to pull away, couldn't pull away. She wanted to feel more of those hot, devouring lips, the only lips she'd ever wanted to feel on hers.

Anyway, he was giving her no chance to draw back, his arms like steel bands round her body. Steely...

strong…yet protective, warm, as if they belonged there, holding her…holding her safe.

She gave herself up to his kiss…for the time being. She would deal with his treachery later.

Much later.

Simon felt her lips softening under his and felt a surge of triumph—and relief. And more—an overwhelming need to taste more of the woman he'd lusted after since the first day he'd met her and had longed for throughout the year and a half they'd been apart.

He could hardly believe she was in his arms again, giving him a second chance…if that was what she was doing. Best not to think about that, but just to enjoy the moment while he had it…because it couldn't last long, not here in full view of the passing traffic.

He let his mouth move seductively over hers, willing her to feel enough to want more later, when they were alone.

And for a while, it seemed it was what she wanted, too, her mouth quivering under his, her tongue even flicking against the searching thrust of his. Tiny whimpering sounds rose from her throat, sending a surge of raw hunger through him.

But when a car swept by, tooting its horn loudly amidst raucous catcalls from youths hanging out the windows, he heard a muffled grunt of protest, felt her body tense, and he quickly rolled off her, grinning impishly, hoping to turn the whole incident into a joke. One he hoped she would go along with.

"That'll teach you to laugh at me," he mocked, attack seeming the best defence. "You didn't expect me to just lie down and take it, did you? After what you did to me, I *deserved* the kiss of life. That tumble scattered my wits."

She sat up, looking flustered and gloriously flushed. And mutinous.

"You—you *fake!* You planned the whole thing!" Indignant as she was trying to sound, her voice was slightly unsteady, betraying her. His kiss hadn't left her cold, that was for sure. "I should have followed my first instinct and pushed you into the canal!"

He waggled a pained eyebrow. "And how would you have felt if I'd hit my skull on one of those boats and *really* knocked myself out? Would you have jumped in to save me, the way I saved you once?"

"You'll never know, will you?" Tossing her head, she scrambled to her feet, brushing herself down with unnecessary vigour before retrieving her bike. "And if I go to the beach with you," she warned, "you'd better behave yourself. You'll be getting us thrown out of Venice."

It'd be worth it, he thought…as long as they both left Venice together…and stayed together. His brow furrowed as he picked up his bike. Was he expecting the impossible? She was free now to pursue her career and achieve her lofty goals without any distractions from a husband or a family. She'd always been determined not to end up like her mother, totally dependent on a man, with no money of her own and no control over her life…and she was equally determined to show her bigoted father that she could successfully make her own way in the world without having to rely on a man.

Maybe she wouldn't even want him back in her life after going through the trauma of losing a child. Would their grievous loss always be a major stumbling block between them, a problem too difficult to resolve?

They rode more cautiously after that, avoiding any personal banter and only passing comments when they saw something worth commenting about.

When they reached the popular beach side of the island, with its grand hotels, mansions and heavier traffic, they had to concentrate even more. Along the shoreline, behind a high wire fence, hundreds of beach huts were lined up in rows on the beach, the sea a sparkle of blue behind them.

"The best beaches belong to the hotels," Simon told her, "but there are other beaches, with facilities you can use at a price. Our concierge arranged a beach hut and sun lounges for us. My treat. A girl who's recuperating from pneumonia could do with some pampering, I reckon."

His treat? "We'll go halves," she insisted, wondering how Simon could afford to spend money the way he'd been doing…travelling across the world to Venice, staying at a fancy hotel on the Lagoon, renting beach huts "at a price." He'd given up neurosurgery nearly two years ago, after damaging his hand, and had worked as a neurologist for only a few months before taking a whole year off to sail round the world as a ship's medic. He couldn't have made a lot of money as a lowly medic, although, being at sea, maybe he'd been able to save most of what he'd earned.

She remembered that he'd made some wise investments as a high-powered neurosurgeon—he'd been thinking of Lily's future. Maybe he'd decided to dip into those. Lily would never need anything from them now. She gulped hard and blinked rapidly, quickly switching her thoughts to her own finances.

A good part of her own salary went to rent, living expenses and smart clothes for work. London was an outrageously expensive place to live. But she'd managed to save a little, hence her splurge here in Venice. They would definitely go halves.

"Let's grab something to eat before we go down to the beach," Simon said. By this time, they were wheeling their bikes, weaving their way through the other day-trippers.

After gaining admittance and securing their bikes, they munched on ham rolls and sipped bottled water as they set off across the grainy, sun-washed sand to their assigned beach hut, wondering how much peace they'd get with so many other people around. The air rang with shouts and squeals of laughter, the sound of a father yelling to his child in the water, the boom and swish of waves gently breaking on the shore.

"I hope you brought your swim togs," said Simon, raising a dark eyebrow. Underneath, his blue eyes glinted, quickening her heartbeat. How long since she'd seen that dangerously sexy-glint?

"I'm wearing them underneath," she admitted, annoyingly aware of a flush rising to her cheeks. Ridiculous to be so be shy with her own husband!

"Great," he said, grinning. "Then let's just peel off and enjoy the sun. Unless you want to change in private?" He waved to the beach hut. "We can soak up the sun for a while and have a dip later, if you don't think the water will be too cold for you."

"Of course not. Why should it? If I can survive a tumble into the Grand Canal in early May, I can swim in the sea in the first week of Italy's summer."

"You hadn't been sick back then. You need to take care. I don't think you've been looking after yourself properly."

Meaning *he* wanted to take care of her? She let her gaze flutter away, hiding the yearning in her eyes. How *could* he mean that, when she lived in London and he must be anxious to get back to Australia, back to the brilliant career he'd put aside for so long. Now he'd had time to recover from the injury to his hand, and had taken that long, healing round-the-world voyage, he must be longing to pick up the threads of his old life again.

"I'm fine," she asserted, and she meant it. The sun, the invigorating bike ride round the island and being with the only man she'd ever wanted, even if it didn't or couldn't last, were doing wonders for her health, her skin, her eyes. She could feel it.

When she glanced up again, he was doing a striptease in front of her. In front of every female on the beach, in fact—and there were plenty of them. First, he unveiled his magnificent torso—the bronzed, well-toned chest, the strong brown arms, the broad shoulders. And then—she swallowed—he peeled off his jeans, stepping out of them with casual ease, exposing his powerful thighs, even more tanned flesh, and brief black trunks that moulded his masculinity like…like…

She tore her eyes away. Next, she'd be panting.

Determined not to hide away in a beach hut, she fumbled with her own clothes, stripping off her sleeveless top first, wishing with a thumping heart that she had a tan to rival his, and more luscious, more womanly curves. She ripped off her ankle-length pants before she could think twice and maybe change her mind. She could feel a prickly heat rising up her face, uncomfortably aware of his eyes on her.

She thought at least he might have looked away, given her some sense of privacy after all this time apart, but no, he was blatantly inspecting her from head to toe, his dark-lashed eyes gleaming blue slits in the sunlight.

"Mmm...nice bikini. You always looked good in a swimsuit."

She couldn't look at him, thankful she was wearing sunglasses and a shady peaked cap as she made a big show of rummaging in her backpack for her sun cream and a towel. He was just trying to make her feel better. He must be. She knew how thin she'd become, and how pale her skin was.

She began to slather her arms and legs with sun cream.

"Lie down on the sun lounge and let me do your back for you," Simon murmured.

It was too tempting an offer to refuse. "If you like," she said, her flippant tone covering a tremor that rippled all the way down to her toes. She lowered herself flat on her stomach on the sun lounge, with a bent arm under her cheek. She could already feel the sun seeping into her skin, her bones, her veins. And other sensations that had nothing to do with the sun.

When his hand first touched her skin, she trembled involuntarily, remembering other touches, more intimate touches... *No! Best not to remember! Just relax, you idiot!* To cover up her reaction, she gasped, "Your

hand's cold! I—I mean the sun cream feels cold!"
Simon's hands were never cold. Even in the depths of
winter, his hands were always warm...warm and...
"Rub it in, quickly!"

"My pleasure." There was a roguish satisfaction in
his voice, as if she hadn't fooled him for a second. "But
I think slowly and carefully would be better."

He began to stroke her back, ever so gently, with the
flat of his hands, the warm, caring hands she'd always
loved. Up...down...up...down...up...over her shoulders...down again...down...

She could feel her body heating, and knew it wasn't
just the effect of the sun or the soothing massage. She
could feel things stirring deep inside that she hadn't felt
for the past two lonely years. Need, desire, longing...

"Now roll over and I'll do your other side."

She nearly jackknifed at the thought of his hands on
the swell of her breasts, stroking over her stomach, her
inner thighs. *Oh dear heaven!* She felt faint at the erotic
images taking shape in her mind. It would be too exquisitely arousing to bear. And even more unbearable to
have to tamp down her rising passion and ignore the
aching need inside her. She could hardly give in to it
here, on a public beach. She was no exhibitionist.

"I can do it!" She jerked around, grabbing the sun
cream from his hand and slapping it over her chest and
stomach. Was he feeling the same burning hunger? Was
that the only reason he'd sought her out after all this
time? Because he missed her in bed, the one place
where they'd been able to connect and transcend their
grief?

Or did he want more than that? Did he *feel* more?

Was he capable of loving again? Only by loving her and sharing his thoughts and his memories of Lily would she know he'd forgiven her at last.

She closed her eyes and let the sun's warmth, rather than Simon's seductive hands, caress her body. She could hear him settling down on the sun lounge beside her, but she didn't peek or speak to him. Let him think she was dozing off, weary after their long bike ride. She needed a few moments to regain her composure.

Simon lay back, a ghost of a smile on his lips. She still wanted him, all right. He'd felt her body burn, could still feel the way she'd trembled under his touch. And the way she'd snatched the sun cream away from him before he could massage her body more intimately...

He had a feeling that tonight could be the night. All they needed was to be alone, somewhere romantic— *hell, anywhere in Venice was romantic!*—and the rest would follow. She would realize she not only wanted his body, but she needed him back in her life, the way he needed her. They would lay their ghosts to rest, and make a brand-new start—and this time they'd make it work. *He* would make it work. *He* would do everything—anything—it took.

Even if it meant reliving their daughter's last traumatic moments and his own regrettable failure. Annabel had been relying on him to save her baby, shockingly injured as their little love was, and he hadn't been able to perform the miracle she'd prayed for.

He let her soak up the sun in mutual silence until the heat on his skin became intense and he decided he'd given her long enough. He didn't want her getting sun-burned and being in too much agony to enjoy a roman-tic night alone with him—should luck be on his side.

"Want a dip in the sea before we bake ourselves to a frizzle?" He spoke softly, in case she'd fallen asleep.

She stirred at once and sat up, making it obvious she'd been as wide awake as he was. He wondered what she'd been thinking about. Him, he hoped. Not... *No! Just think about now...being here together.*

"Sounds good," she said, removing her cap and sun-glasses. "As long as you don't challenge me to a race. You've probably had lots of sneaky practice, being at sea for so long."

'I wish you'd been with me," he said without think-ing. *Oh sure...you would hardly have been good com-pany, Pacino...at least for the first few months, sunk in a black pit with your demons.* He shook off the un-wanted memory. That was all in the past. The sea, the tough new challenges he'd had to face and the passing weeks with other things to do and think about had even-tually spun their healing magic.

He tried to paint a picture of what it was like. "It was another world out there...the open sea all around us, the endless sky, wild storms, raw nature and the elements. And unimaginable beauty. We called into some fasci-nating foreign ports and one or two uninhabited is-lands—true deserted islands. It was a complete change from anything I'd ever done before. I reckon you'd have loved it."

He half expected her to snap back, *How could I af-ford to take a year off, swanning around the world? I'd never get a partnership that way.* But instead, he saw her eyes turn dreamy for a second, and she said rather wistfully, "It sounds wonderful." She was already on her feet. "Beat you down to the water!"

"You're on." He took off after her, dodging bodies and small children on the way.

The water was refreshing, if crowded with other tourists and not brilliantly clean. There was no hope of having a race, or even a proper swim, with so many other bathers around. But they splashed and bobbed around, and laughed a lot, just as they had on their honeymoon.

It felt good to see her laughing again, and it felt surprisingly good to be able to laugh himself. Laughter was healing, the medical pundits said. He sure hoped they were right.

They were still laughing when they ran up the beach and snatched up their towels.

"Well, that washed a few cobwebs away!" Annabel flicked her towel over herself and began rubbing her dripping hair. She felt breathless, and not just from the swim and the run up the beach. Breathless from…excitement. A giddy expectation of the promise of even better things to come.

"If you had any cobwebs, I didn't see them," Simon said, his natural gallantry coming to the fore. "You look wonderful. Spending a day at the beach has done you a power of good. You're not feeling overtired?"

"Heck, no. I feel invigorated." For a second she let her eyes drink in the sight of him—her Italian Romeo, as she'd first thought of him four years ago—standing there like a bold, strapping gladiator, water glistening on his bare tanned chest, his powerful legs stretched wide on the sand as he dabbed at his wet hair with a towel.

Today had been good…had done wonders…in more ways than one.

"Let's dry off for a few minutes in the sun," said Simon, flopping down onto his sun lounge, "and then you can get dressed in the privacy of our beach hut. Think you can face another bike ride back to the *vaporetto*? The direct route this time, no detours."

"No worries. As long as you behave yourself and don't go careering into canals."

"As long as *I* behave? That's rich! Who stopped without warning?"

"You shouldn't have been so close," she retorted, grinning. It felt good—amazingly liberating—to be able to spar with each other again, and lightheartedly tease each other. Something she'd never believed would be possible again.

This new easy rapport between them emboldened her to ask the question she'd held back for so long…or at least to carefully lead up to the vital question. "How's your hand standing up to all this use and abuse?"

"My hand? Oh, no problem." He held it up, bent it sideways and wiggled it up and down. "It's better."

"You're not just putting on a brave face? It's really better?"

He held it out to her. "Here, take it. Examine it. Do what you like with it."

What she liked with it… She felt her own hand shaking as she took possession of his, feeling its warmth, its texture, its strength. *Oh, Simon, if you only knew what*

I'd like to do with it. She thrust it away with an unsteady laugh. "Look, I believe you. You're the doctor, not me. If you say it's better…"

"It is." There was amusement in his voice. Maybe he'd felt her hand trembling under his. Yes, he'd love that. Knowing what he did to her.

Did it matter if he knew? Hadn't she shown him enough times already that he only had to touch her… She gulped, switching her mind back to the real question she wanted to ask him.

"Well, now that your hand's better…really better… and now that you've had your year off, sailing the high seas…" Heck, this was difficult. But she pressed on. "Will you be going back to your surgical career when you leave Venice?"

A curtain seemed to drop between them. She felt it immediately, regretted the question in the same breath. It was too soon to ask. He still wasn't ready.

"No." His reply came after a painfully long moment. He wasn't looking at her. His glinting blue eyes were narrowed, their expression hidden under dark, lowered brows. "I've given up neurosurgery. I made my decision over a year ago. I won't change my mind."

He was slipping away from her again. She could feel it. In desperation, she took the bull by the horns. She wasn't going to let him…not this time.

"But it's the only thing you've ever wanted to do!" *Make him talk about it. Don't let him shut you out again.* "And you've so much to offer. You're so good at it…the best…everyone says so…" That was the wrong thing to say, too. She sensed it in the stiffening of his body, the sudden chill in the air.

"Not good enough."

Because he hadn't been able to save Lily.

The unspoken thought hung between them. "You can't blame yourself!" she cried, appalled. She didn't have to mention their daughter's name. He'd know who she meant. "There was no hope, you must have known that. She was beyond help…anyone's help…all the doctors said so. But being the brilliant surgeon you are, you insisted on trying. You did your best…" *And when you failed to save her, you were gutted and blamed me, though you never accused me to my face. You probably still blame me…*

"I had to try," he muttered. "There was no one else available but an inexperienced registrar, and time was running out. I would never have operated on my own child otherwise, would never have been *allowed* to. But I was her best hope, her *only* hope." He gave an impatient shrug, hiding the agony she knew he was still feeling. "Look, this isn't the time or the place to go into this, Bel. I've given up neurosurgery and that's it. There are plenty of other things I can do."

He didn't say what, and she didn't ask. If she persisted, he might shut her out altogether, the way he had before.

She felt a rush of sympathy for him, understanding him as never before. He couldn't face doing neurosurgery any more because it reminded him of Lily and how his skills, expert as everyone said they were, hadn't been able to save her. He was taking responsibility for their daughter's death to cover up the fact that he secretly blamed *her*—his wife—for letting the accident happen in the first place. He was doing his best to blot out the painful truth, to put what happened behind him, because he still felt something for her.

She still wasn't sure quite what. Or just how deep his feelings went. But at least they'd both taken a few small steps forward. They'd begun to communicate…a little…and not only with their bodies. She just had to be patient.

And hope their feelings for each other would be strong enough to repair the shattered fragments of their lives and give them the chance to put them back together again.

"I'd better go and get dressed," she said, unfurling her sun-warmed body and making a dive for the changing hut.

"Call me if you need any help." The roguish note was back in his voice.

What a relief it was to hear it! With a lighter heart, she called back, somehow injecting a mock tartness into her tone, "I can manage, thank you very much!"

She was sure she heard a murmured "Pity" float back.

Chapter Six

It was late afternoon by the time they arrived back in Venice. Annabel was more than ready to get back to the hotel and indulge in a bit of personal pampering—showering, washing her hair, painting her nails, choosing something sexy to wear for the evening—before meeting Simon again for dinner.

"You go ahead." Simon touched her shoulder for a second—just long enough for her to feel the alluring heat of his hand. "I need to find an American Express office and change some traveler's checks. There's one near St. Mark's Square. Meet around seven-thirty in the bar? We can decide where to eat then. Or just wander out and take potluck."

"Let's take potluck," she said as they exchanged smiles—it warmed her heart to see him smiling so readily again—before parting ways.

It took only a few minutes to reach the hotel. As she asked for her key at the desk, Giorgio handed her a wad of messages.

"There have been many phone calls for you, *signora*," he said in his heavily accented English. "All from London. Your office want you to call them as soon as you come in. I could not say when you would be back," he added apologetically.

"Thank you, Giorgio," she said, glancing at the scribbled phone messages in her hand. Most of them were from her secretary Elizabeth, the rest—the last two—from Ambrose, the senior partner. They all had the same blunt message. *Call the office immediately. You're needed back here.*

She hurried to the lifts, an inner qualm drawing a frown. Why would they be wanting her back at the office so urgently? The worst scenario she could think of was that they'd grown tired of her being sick and taking time off and had decided to get rid of her.

Her throat seized up. But they couldn't! Not now, when she was so close to achieving her longed-for goal. A couple of the partners had dropped hints recently...though not since she'd been sick. *Oh dear heaven...*

She tried to stifle her fears as she rode up in the lift. It was probably just a work-related matter, to do with a past case she'd been dealing with...some problem she had to handle personally. No need to panic.

Her fingers fumbled with her key before she managed to open her door. She dropped her backpack on the bed, threw the messages onto the desk, and picked up the phone with shaking fingers. She asked for Elizabeth rather than Ambrose. Better if Liz prepared her first.

When she came on the line Liz wasted no time on pleasantries. "Ah, Annabel, at last! We've been trying to get you all day. You're going to have to rush or you'll miss your flight."

Annabel gripped the phone. "Flight? Rush? You mean you want me back in London *now? Tonight?*" She had visions of having to leave Simon before they'd had a chance to resolve things between them. *Oh please, no, not yet.* "What's going on, Liz? Why the panic?" What if Simon failed to turn up before she had to leave for the airport, denying her the chance to explain or even say goodbye?

"There wouldn't have been a panic if you'd called a bit sooner. Or had your cell phone with you." Liz sounded harassed—unusual for the usually unflappable Elizabeth.

"Sorry, Liz." Annabel thought of all the calls the poor girl had had to make and felt sympathy for her. "I spent the day at the Lido and didn't think I'd need my cell phone. So what's up?"

"Mr. Mallaby's arriving tonight from Sydney!" Liz spoke in the awed tone she would have used to announce the imminent arrival of the Queen. "He's called a meeting for first thing in the morning and he wants you to be there." Her tone clearly said, *When the senior partner from our Sydney head office says jump, you jump.*

"Oh," was all Annabel could manage. Why, she wondered, was it so important for her to be at this meeting? Unless it really *was* the worst kind of news. Would Guy Mallaby himself, the man who'd first employed her, come all the way from Australia to give her the sack personally? *Oh no, it can't be that! It couldn't end like this!*

She could already see her father's smugly self-satisfied face, could already hear him taunting her. *So you thought you could make it in a man's world? Ha! I did try to warn you. A woman's place is in the home, with her husband and children. It's what a woman is best fitted for. Now perhaps you'll see sense.*

She shook herself as her own common sense took over. Would they recall her so urgently simply to sack her? Would Guy Mallaby come all this way, just for that? *Get real, Annabel.* What if it was *good* news? The best possible news? What if they were about to offer her a partnership? She sucked in a reviving breath.

"You're booked on the 6 p.m. flight from Venice." The urgency in Liz's voice burst the bubble of her rising excitement. "To make it, you'll have to check out of the hotel straight away, grab a water taxi and head straight for the airport. Okay?"

Straight away..."Okay," Annabel echoed, her voice a thin thread of sound. *Straight away* meant no time even for a shower, let alone any pampering. "I'm on my way." Her head was spinning as she hung up and pulled out her suitcase. If only she *had* taken her cell phone with her to the Lido today. She would have known hours ago. Simon would have known, too, and they could have prepared themselves...talked about it. Now it was too late. *Oh Simon...*

She was all packed, changed and heading for the lift within minutes. As she handed over her credit card at the desk downstairs, she cast a hopeful look around. But there was still no sign of Simon, either in the lobby or in the bar beyond. Unless he'd slipped up to his room already.

After asking Giorgio to summon a water taxi, she picked up a guest phone and dialed Simon's room number. No answer. Damn!

"Would you leave a message for Simon Pacino, Giorgio?" she asked him with a wobbly smile. "Please tell him I had to return to London urgently. I'll call him from the airport." *If she had time.* The plane was due to leave at six o'clock. She would barely make the flight.

But what if she did find time to call and he still wasn't back? Or was in the shower and not answering his phone? How could she contact him later, from London, if he'd decided by then to leave Venice, too? If he possessed a cell phone, she'd never seen it. There'd be no way to reach him.

But at least he would know how to reach *her.* He'd called her London office before. She just hoped he wouldn't think she'd run out on him again, and not bother to chase after her a second time. Her heart dipped.

"The water taxi is waiting for you, *signora,*" Giorgio said. She thanked him, waved away an offer of help with her bag and hurried to the rear exit, where a narrow canal brought boats to the door. She could feel her tension building as the motorboat whisked her across the Lagoon.

Would Simon care enough about her to seek her out again? Or would he take her sudden flight as a sign that she didn't want to see any more of him? As confirmation that her job, her high-powered career, was all she cared about?

Was it? *Did* it still come first, before anything or anyone else? It always had in the past, she realized painfully. But so had Simon's career…once. They'd both been equally driven, equally ambitious, equally determined to reach their sought-after goals. She still couldn't believe that Simon had put his own cherished career behind him and given up neurosurgery forever.

She slumped a little, her heart aching for him. If she knew Simon, he would never be completely happy again if he gave up surgery for good. It was his life, and he'd always loved it. And he was brilliant at it.

At least he'd turned the first corner in getting his life back. He'd taken the time to heal his physical and emotional wounds, and then he'd come looking for her. He was smiling and joking again, and acting more like his old self. He'd even talked about the loss of their daughter…to a point.

She cast a pensive look back across the Lagoon to the domes and spires of the Venetian skyline. Somewhere, back there, Simon was in blissful ignorance of her sudden departure, maybe indulging in erotic dreams of a romantic evening together. *Oh, Simon…what will you think when you find out I've gone?*

If he thought she'd decided to put her job, her ambition before a new life with him and that her work was more important to her than he was—she bit her lip, her eyes narrowing—maybe he would start thinking of his own needs, finally. Maybe he would even begin to get his old drive and enthusiasm back, and decide to return to his own brilliant career, where he belonged…in neurosurgery.

She hoped he *would* go back. It was the work he loved, and where he excelled, despite that one tragic blow to his perfect record. And he must know that Lily's death had been no fault of his...that his wife alone was to blame. She was the one who'd taken Lily out in her pram on that tragic Sunday.

He clearly *did* know, deep down, and the thought of it had plainly shattered him and shut him off from her and the world. But since spending a year at sea, he'd pulled himself out of his dark void and he seemed finally to have come to terms with what she'd done, to have put the trauma of two years ago behind him, or at least the worst of it. He was well on the way to being the old dynamic Simon she'd longed to see again, and his next step, hopefully, would see him returning to his beloved profession.

She had her hand on her cell phone, ready to call him again at the hotel, to explain her sudden recall to London, but with a sigh she let her hand drop. She turned her face into the wind, feeling it bring a sting of tears to her eyes. *Oh, Simon, I love you so much...and that's why I have to let you go. You'll thank me one day...when you have your life back.*

If she called him now and invited him to follow her to London, just to be with her, to give *her* support, he might never go back to surgery. He'd be more likely to settle for second best, for a safe, undemanding, unfulfilling job simply so they could spend more time together.

If he did still care for her—and would he have followed her to Venice if he didn't?—she could imagine him making that sacrifice, giving up his own career and the fulfillment of his own dreams for hers, to make their marriage work. And she couldn't let it happen.

Tears blurred her eyes, and this time they weren't from the wind. Even if it meant losing him again, denying her own aching need for him, she had to give him this chance to resurrect his career.

It needn't be forever. Once he was safely back in neurosurgery, where he was meant to be, and she was secure enough in her job to request a transfer back to Australia—hopefully as a fully-fledged partner—they could get back together again. With her seeking *him* out next time.

A tremulous smile brushed her lips. They would both have what they'd always wanted. Their ambitions realized...and each other.

She would cling to that dream.

Simon cursed the long delay at the American Express office. Had every tourist in Venice decided to change traveler's checks at the same time? And why were they all taking so damned long? He needed a shower. He needed a change of clothes. He needed to see Annabel again, so he could wine and dine her and then take her somewhere quiet and romantic and sweep her off her feet.

His lip quirked at his pleasant daydream. Was he reading too much into a snatched kiss, a few shared laughs, and her warm body quivering under his hands? She'd been that way with him on their first romantic encounter in Venice, yet she'd left him without a backward glance to pursue her independent life and her soaring career back in Australia. It was only her unplanned pregnancy that had brought them back together again.

He shrugged off his qualms. It was different this time. They'd both changed, matured since their shared tragedy. They were fully aware of the mistakes they'd made, the inadequate time they'd allowed for each other in the ruthless pursuit of their dreams. This time, they wouldn't both have demanding, conflicting careers to rule their lives and keep them constantly apart. With only one challenging career to consider, he could support her, give her his time, make life easier for her. Even ensure they made time for some fun.

He wouldn't be missing out. He had an idea about what he wanted to do himself and it would give him normal hours, fewer demands and less stress on their marriage. He might even tell her tonight. It was time they started to really talk to each other. Even if it meant talking about other things in his life…deeper, darker things that he'd never been able to face.

He felt the old hollowness inside and heaved in a savage breath. If they were going to have any chance at all, she would have to know the worst about him, that there was something else as bad as…Lily. The shock of his daughter's death had dredged it up from the dark place where he'd hidden it away all these years, blocking it out of his mind, out of his life, as if it had never happened.

The worst, most monstrous act of his life.

For his own peace of mind and for the sake of their marriage, he would have to find a way to tell her…to let her know it was more than just Lily's death tormenting him, causing him to shut her out in that unforgivable way. If he didn't face up to his darkest, most shameful sin, it would always be there between them.

Sharing his dark family secret, exposing his deepest scars, was a risk he would have to take…even if it shocked and disgusted her and drove her away again.

He couldn't go on hiding it, pretending it never happened, living a lie.

"*Signor?*"

"Oh. Sorry. *Scusi.*" The queue in front of him had magically dissolved. He stepped forward, carried out his transactions and escaped into the open air.

In the narrow, crowded alleys the shadows were lengthening, the air cooling. There were even a few gray clouds. He hoped they weren't rain clouds. When it rained in Venice, it could really bucket down, flooding the city before you knew it. Annabel hadn't come to Venice to get wet feet and catch a chill. She'd come here to drink in the sun and get her health back.

Today had done wonders for her. Her pearly skin had glowed with healthy colour after their hours in the sun. He could still feel its silky softness under his fingers as he'd rubbed in the sun cream. It had taken all his willpower not to drop down on top of her then and there, and slide his aroused body over hers.

It aroused him again now just to think about it.

He dodged his way back along the *Riva,* pausing only to buy a colorful novelty jester for Annabel from a tourist stall laden with trinkets. It might amuse her.

The thought of seeing her again made him impatient to freshen up and change. Time was flying by, and he needed a thorough cleanup, from his salt-clogged hair to his sand-encrusted toes. He wanted to look good and smell good...for *her.* He had a feeling they were going to end up in one of their rooms tonight...he wasn't fussed which one. He just wanted to finish what he'd started on the grassy bank of that canal...to take up where his lips had left off.

She'd given him the green light then, and again on the beach when she couldn't stop her body from trembling beneath his hands. She'd shown that she still wanted him...maybe as much as he wanted her.

His spirits soared at the thought, his steps quickening as he neared the hotel. They'd always been good together...that way, at least. Even after...he blew out a sigh...even during the blackest time of their married life. But their hearts and minds hadn't been involved in those last traumatic months together. Only physical feeling...sensation...release.

Now, hopefully, it would be different, because they would be giving each more than just...sex. They would be connecting again at an emotional level...heart, body and soul. It would be like it was when they were first married...with the promise of even better things to come.

As long as they were careful this time.

His step faltered, a coldness brushing his neck. To make the same mistake again could be fatal. Much as they'd both loved their daughter, they hadn't been ready for children four years ago, and they still weren't, with Annabel still chasing her cherished goal, still trying to break through the glass ceiling. He wasn't ready himself, even without his old surgery demands to preoccupy him and take up his time. He needed to face up to his unresolved traumas before he could face up to a future with...another child.

A child was precious...a full-time commitment. A lesson they'd learned too late, and too cruelly. If they ever did decide to have another child, it would be planned next time...planned, longed for and enjoyed to the full, with both of them able to give the time and the love a child deserved.

He strode into the hotel lobby and headed for the desk to collect his room key. When Giorgio looked up and saw him, a look of relief swept over his swarthy face.

"Ah, *Signor* Pacino. I have a message for you. From the young *signora* you had dinner with last night."

"From Annabel?" he asked, and heard the sharpness in his voice. Was there something wrong with her? Was she too tired or too sunburned to meet him tonight? Had he exhausted her today? Had she had a relapse? Oh God, he would never forgive himself if she'd come down with pneumonia again!

"*Si.*" Giorgio spread his hands. "*Signora* Hansen had to return urgently to London."

"She's gone back to *London?*" He couldn't believe it. "Did she say why?"

Giorgio shook his head. "There were *molto* messages from her office. All day. They ask her to come. *Pronto!*" His face screwed up in thought. "She made a call to London, then checked out. She was in much hurry, to catch the six o'clock flight." He brightened. "She say, uh, she will call you from the airport."

Simon glanced at his watch. It was almost six now. "I'll be in my room," he said, taking off in the direction of the lift. "Put the call through when it comes. *Grazie*, Giorgio."

He didn't hold out much hope. She was probably already on board the plane. *Damn it, no, she wouldn't just leave without even trying to call him.* He hissed in his breath as he bounded into the lift, only releasing it when he burst into his room.

There was no flashing light on the phone, no messages. He paced about, waiting, his blood pressure rising.

No call came. He glowered at the silent phone. Her plane must have left by now.

He started making excuses for her. She'd run out of time. It was a wonder she'd even made it to the airport in time. Messages had been coming from London all day, according to Giorgio, but she hadn't been here to get them. That wasn't her fault. It must have been a frantic rush for her, packing, checking out, then making a dash for the airport to catch the six o'clock flight.

He stomped into the bathroom and switched on the shower. He wasn't in the mood for hot water, and turned on the cold. The shock of the icy water came as a welcome diversion.

But not for long. Damn it, couldn't she at least have scribbled him a personal note before she left the hotel? Just a few words in her own writing would have helped. *Sorry I have to rush off, but I can't ignore a summons from on high. It was great being together again. Why don't you join me in London?*

Anything!

Anything but this deafening silence, this feeling of being discarded, forgotten, walked out on...just like the last time she'd run out on him. He felt a deep slow anger boiling inside him. She didn't care about him. She only cared about her precious high-powered career. She'd only ever cared about fighting her way to the top, becoming a partner to prove herself equal to the men, to show her father that a woman had the same rights and talents as a man...a sentiment he'd always fully agreed with, backing her to the hilt.

But there were other things in life. He'd learned that the hard way. And he, at least, had come to see the light.

He'd thought, in these past couple of days, that she was beginning to feel the same, to want to ease back a bit, enjoy life a bit more. *Their* life, his and hers. Maybe even to start anew, the two of them together...taking care to avoid the mistakes they'd made before.

He scowled as he threw on some clothes without caring what he chose or what he looked like. *The two of them together?* Ha! The moment her precious law firm crooked its little finger, she was off. And he was forgotten.

Snatching up his key, he slammed out of the room and made a beeline for the bar.

Annabel dressed with care the next morning, choosing a gray pin-striped power suit with a crisp white blouse. She pulled on sheer dark stockings and shiny black shoes...with sensible heels. When you're competing with the men, you'd be mad to risk alienating them by flaunting your feminine attributes in the office. Smart yet attractive was the order of the day. Looking competent and efficient—which she hoped she was.

She hoped she didn't look nervous, as well. Having no idea what to expect of this morning's meeting, she was a mass of butterflies inside. She had the jittery feeling that her future was about to be decided. But whether the news was going to be good or bad, she wasn't game to hazard a guess.

To make things worse, she couldn't stop thinking about Simon, about how he must have reacted when he found out she'd gone, when he realized she'd put her job first again. Would he be understanding, knowing how much her career meant to her? Or would he feel angry and fed up and wipe his hands of her?

Angry... She froze at the thought. He'd lost his temper the first time she'd run out on him, and he'd wrecked his hand and his career. *Oh dear heaven, what have I done?* If he "lost it" again, did himself another injury, he could lose any chance of going back to neurosurgery, where, in his heart, he must long to be. Far from heading back to Sydney to resume his career, as she'd been hoping he would, he'd be more likely to turn away from it altogether.

And it would all be her fault.

She glared in repugnance at her smart businesslike image in the full-length mirror. Why hadn't she called Simon from the airport, or from her flat last night? Or scribbled a brief personal note before she left? Just to let him know how sorry she was for leaving so abruptly and how much she'd loved their few days together. Leaving the door open. Lifting his spirits instead of crushing them, leaving him high and dry.

Now it was too late.

Late? Oh heck! She jerked back to life. If she didn't hurry, she'd be late for this meeting with Guy Mallaby.

She snatched up her handbag and fled.

Chapter Seven

When she walked into the office, Liz grabbed her.

"Ah, Annabel, you made it. Feeling better? You look great. The break's obviously done wonders." The girl didn't wait for an answer. "Mr. Mallaby wants to see you in the boardroom…now, before the meeting gets under way."

Annabel's heart sank. Why would he want to see her alone…*before* the meeting? It had to be bad news. He wanted to tell her personally, one-on-one…let her down lightly. And then he'd let the partners know she'd be leaving.

She hissed in an indignant breath. She'd left Simon…left Venice early…for *this*?

"Right. Thanks, Liz." She forced a smile as she turned away, forced her legs to carry her toward the boardroom. She would face Guy Mallaby with her head held high. There were plenty of other law firms that would snap her up. Law firms back in Australia. In Sydney.

Would Simon go back to Sydney? She no longer felt confident that he would. Even if he went back to neurosurgery, he'd never go back to the same hospital, the one where... No, it would hold too many painful memories. But she could always find out where he was. If he *did* go back to his old career.

Did dreams, hopes, wishes, ever come true? *I'll never go back to neurosurgery,* he'd vowed only yesterday. What if he reacted badly to her walking out on him again and stuck to his vow? He—he could end up anywhere...doing anything. Sailing the high seas again, for all she would know.

Oh, Simon, I've really messed up, haven't I?

She jutted her chin as she knocked on the boardroom door. Whatever happened to *her,* it couldn't be worse than what she'd done to Simon. She could take whatever was coming. Whatever they threw at her.

"Come in. Ah... Annabel." Guy Mallaby rose from the boardroom table as she walked in. Tall and still handsome in his fifties, his face gave nothing away. He had a pile of papers in front of him. Were some for her to sign? Severance papers? She tilted her chin a notch higher.

Instead of shaking her hand, he gripped her shoulders and examined her face. She had to look up at him... he'd always been a towering, impressive figure. His charcoal hair was turning silver above his ears, giving him an even more distinguished air than the last time she'd seen him. His brown eyes were warm and...sympathetic? Was he feeling sorry for what he was about to do?

"I was sorry to hear you've been ill, my dear, and more than sorry I had to cut short your recuperation in Venice. It's obviously done you good…you're looking wonderful."

"Thank you, Mr. Mallaby. Yes, I'm fine now." Was this the soft soap before the hammer fell?

"Good, good. Unfortunate that I had to rush you back, but I only have one day here in London, then I have to fly to Zurich for some meetings, then back to Sydney the next day. I wanted you here so I could tell you myself."

Definitely sympathy. She faced him bravely, without blinking. She would take it like a man…on the chin. She'd learned long ago that when you competed with men, you needed to be strong. You needed to be even better, tougher, cleverer than they were. She could thank her father's bigoted attitude to women for making her strong in the first place. She needed that strength now.

"I've heard nothing but good reports about you, Annabel. Your contribution to Mallaby's has been exemplary. Brilliant." My, he *was* letting her down lightly. "You've been a dedicated, hardworking, reliable member of the team…a real asset to the firm. I hear you even kept on working when you first fell ill. No wonder you ended up with pneumonia. You jeopardized your health for Mallaby's."

He paused a moment, and she held her breath. *This is it.* "We'd like to reward you by promoting you from an associate to a full partner, Annabel."

She had been so psyched up to hear the worst, she

couldn't take it in for a second. Her head was spinning. "S-sorry?" Maybe she hadn't heard right.

"We'd like to make you a partner, Annabel. And we want you back in the Sydney office. Your time here in London has given you valuable experience, but I always intended to bring you back to Australia. Will you consider our offer?"

Now her head was doing more than spinning; it was in orbit, whirling into space. A partner…back in Sydney! Her lifelong ambition realized. Her years of hard work rewarded. Her longed-for dream come true.

And Simon wasn't here to share this dreamed-about moment with her.

It was like a dash of cold water. He'd backed her, encouraged her from the beginning, rejoiced with her at each promotion on her way up. But what must he be thinking of her now, after being callously abandoned for a second time? He must feel that her career, her single-minded ambition, had ripped them asunder.

She squeezed her hands together, convinced he would be cursing the high-powered career she'd chosen.

Yet if it sent him back to his own career…the career he'd always loved with a passion…

"Annabel?"

She jumped guiltily. And blew out a relieved breath when she saw that Mallaby was smiling, looking more amused than irritated.

"I—I don't know what to say." *Oh heck, listen to her stammering like an idiot. What was wrong with her? She'd imagined this moment for years, rehearsed the gracious little speech she would make. Why wasn't she saying it?*

"It's the first time I've seen you speechless, Annabel." The benign smile stretched wider. "I thought you
would have been expecting it. Look, you don't have to
give me an answer right now. It's something you must
think about, take your time weighing the pros and cons.
Whether you accept or not, we want you back in the
Sydney office. We can discuss terms and conditions
there. How soon can you come back? Would another
two days give you long enough to tie things up here?"

Two days! She gulped. The apartment and the packing would be no problem—the flat belonged to one of
the partners and because it had come already furnished,
she had few possessions to worry about. But she'd have
a bit of paperwork to catch up on, clients and banks to
notify, some legal work to tie up, air tickets to organ-
ize. It would mean working long hours, with little rest
in the evenings.

"No problem," she said, somehow reclaiming her
usual confident air, her tone crisply efficient. "Thank
you for the offer, Mr. Mallaby," she added belatedly.
"I'm...honored." And she was...even though she'd
worked hard for it, *deserved* it, making difficult sacrifices along the way. She thought of the meager time
she'd allowed for Lily—"quality time," she'd loftily
called it, but she knew now it hadn't been good enough.
Lily had deserved more. Her parents had been right
about that, at least.

Her parents... She must let them know she was coming back to Australia—and casually let drop that she'd
been offered a partnership. Maybe then they would realize that a woman could make it to the top of a male-
dominated profession, and be proud of her, happy for her.

And pigs might fly.

"I think you could call me Guy, Annabel...*all the other partners do.*" All the other partners... He was already including her in the elite circle. "You'll sit in at our meeting in a few minutes...and we'll let them know you're transferring back to Sydney...with a partnership on offer."

She nodded, feeling a stir of excitement as it sank in at last. She'd made it! She'd reached her goal, broken through the legendary glass ceiling, soared to the moon. It was hard to take in, hard to believe.

Yet...

She should have been on cloud nine, floating on air, wanting to shout out loud with joy, but something was missing. *Simon.* Simon, the man she loved, her *husband,* wasn't a part of it.

What if she changed her mind and did tell him, after all...assuming she could still find him? Knowing she'd finally reached her goal might be just the fillip he needed to fire up his own ambition. And hearing that she would be coming back to Sydney...that they would still be able to see each other...and maybe even...

But she was getting ahead of herself. He could have left Venice already, be lost to her already. But dammit, she could *try.* The moment the partners' meeting was over, she would slip into her office and call the hotel in Venice, find out if he was still booked in there.

She longed to share her news with him, longed to hear his voice again, longed to beg him: *Let's meet up again back in Sydney.*

Simon caught an early flight out of Venice, having checked out of the hotel without bothering about breakfast. He felt like death after a heavy night at the bar, but he'd done a lot of thinking during the early hours, as he tossed about in his bed, his thoughts swinging this way and that until he'd finally made up his mind about what he was going to do.

He would probably regret it, but he might live to regret it more if he didn't take the chance. *Follow your heart,* his mother had always told him. And this was where his heart lay. His heart and his future.

He had to give it another try.

Mallaby's London office took up the whole of the third floor of what was known as The Tower, a five-story modern building in South Kensington. Late into the evening, with everyone else gone, it was eerily quiet on the third floor.

Annabel, working alone in her office, wasn't nervous. She knew that nobody could get into the building without pressing a buzzer at the front door and gaining admission from the security guard in the foyer down below. At least one person had come and gone already. Feeling hungry as the evening went on, she'd sent out for a pizza to keep her going, and a fresh-faced delivery boy had brought it up to her in the lift. The coffee machine had kept her going since.

But now, finally, she called it a night. She'd made a hole in her towering In basket and tied up some other loose ends, and felt satisfied with her evening's work. Tomorrow night, she'd have to pack up her things at the apartment, ready to send them back to Australia. At lunchtime the next day—her last day in London—her work colleagues were taking her out for farewell drinks;

by the evening, she'd be on a plane. The next two days would pass in no time.

Everyone at Mallaby's had seemed genuinely happy for her, and the excitement and acclamation might have gone to her head if she hadn't been missing Simon so much. She couldn't stop thinking about him, finding it hard to concentrate on her work, wondering what he must be thinking of her after the way she'd run out on him. Again.

He must hate her. He hadn't hung around in Venice for her call. He must have wiped his hands of her. The receptionist at the Gabrielli had dashed her last hope of speaking to him and trying to explain. He'd checked out early that morning.

It cast a shadow over a day that should have been perfect, turning the promotion she'd been offered into a hollow triumph.

She had to remind herself that this was the outcome she'd wanted. For Simon to be free to think of his own future…for him to go back to Australia, rediscover his old enthusiasm and decide to resume his career in neurosurgery.

They would meet up again one day…one day *soon*. They would!

She gathered up her handbag and briefcase and rode down in the lift. When she stepped out at the ground floor, she blinked in disbelief. For a second she thought her imagination, or some fanciful daydream, had conjured up the figure sprawled half-asleep on the wooden bench opposite the lifts.

She blinked and looked again, and he was still there. Large as life.

The man she most wanted to see.

The man she'd convinced herself she *didn't* want to see. He was supposed to be on his way back to Australia, free to pick up the pieces of his own career...to fulfill his own lifelong dream.

She found her voice—somehow. "Simon! What on earth are you doing here?"

He opened his eyes, stretched his cramped muscles and hauled himself rather unsteadily to his feet. "Waiting for you."

She ran forward and grabbed him by the arm, afraid he was going to keel over. At least he seemed to be in one piece. No sign of self-inflicted injury or broken bones. No sign of having "lost it". *Thank heaven.*

"You look half-asleep on your feet!" And maybe a bit under the weather? If he'd been drinking, *she* would have driven him to it. She gripped him a little tighter. It felt so wonderful to touch him again, to feel his warmth under her fingers. "How long have you been here? Why didn't you come up?"

She still couldn't believe he was here, that he'd sought her out again, after the way she'd left him stranded in Venice. *Unless it was just to bid her a final goodbye. Oh, no, please, no.*

She noticed his bulging backpack lying on the floor, as if he hadn't booked in anywhere. *Because he didn't intend to stay?*

"I was told you were still working and I didn't want to interrupt you. I was watching out for you when everyone left work, the first ones around four o'clock." He gave a rueful smile. *He'd been here since four?* "When you didn't appear, I asked the security guard, who said you were still up in your office and did I want him to let you know. I said not to bother you and told him I'd wait down here until you'd finished your work."

"Have you eaten?" she asked, shaking her head. All those hours, sitting on a hard bench! Waiting for *her*.

"Nope. Have you?"

"I had something brought in. Oh, Simon, you must be starving. You'd better come home with me. I'll make you something." Luckily, she'd shopped for a few basic supplies last night on her way home from the airport. "I don't think a bar or a restaurant is the place for you right now. You need somewhere more comfortable, where you can relax. Followed by a good night's sleep."

Oh heck, what was she saying? A good night's sleep...where? In her flat? On the tiny two-seater in the lounge, which would be barely big enough even for her? Or in the double bed...with her?

She felt a tremor and squashed it, remembering the way she'd run out on him without even leaving a note. Without even calling when she reached London. Was he going to be roaring mad at her when he had her alone, and tell her he'd had enough? How would he react if she told him that Guy Mallaby had offered her a partnership and a transfer back to their head office in Sydney? Would he be pleased for her, or would he assume she wouldn't need him or want him in her life, that her career was always going to be self-centered and all-consuming, and finish with her once and for all?

Would it be a good thing for *him*, for his own future, if he did?

Oh Simon, I just want you to be happy, doing what you love most! But I want us to be together, too…once you have your own life back.

She tried to put her qualms aside as she steered him toward the exit. *Just take it a minute at a time, a step at a time. Get him home and fed first.*

"My apartment's just around the corner…walking distance," she said, making a right turn as they left the building. "It belongs to one of the partners." *One of the partners…* Soon she would be one, too. It still felt strange. Unreal. It still hadn't really sunk in.

"I hope you like eggs," she said, bringing her mind back to more practical matters. "I don't have too much on offer, having just got back. It all happened so quickly," she rushed on rather breathlessly, wanting him to understand. "The office tried all day yesterday to get me, to recall me for an urgent meeting this morning. They'd booked me on the six o'clock flight. I barely had time to think, let alone—"

"Let alone leave a note for me, rather than a second-hand message."

He *is* mad at me, she thought in dismay, hearing the weary note in his voice. "I—I intended to ring you from the airport," she said weakly.

"But you ran out of time." It wasn't even a question. He thought she'd had her mind so fixed on London she'd forgotten him. *Oh Simon, it was you I was thinking of, only you.* "Not to worry," he drawled, "I was late getting back to the hotel. It was after six. I wouldn't have been there to take your call." He didn't even bother to mention later in the evening, when she could have called from London, or left a message to call her back if he wasn't there. "Look, we'd better sprint. It's starting to rain."

She obediently broke into a trot, glad of the diversion. "Early summer in London," she quipped. Yeah… she was back in London, all right. But she wouldn't be here for long. She was going back to Australia! Back to *Sydney*… Surely he'd be pleased about *that*.

Simon noted the signs of a hasty departure as they entered her one-bedroom apartment on the first floor of an elegant double-storey apartment block. A half-filled coffee mug on the kitchen bench. An open cornflakes packet on the sink. A dirty breakfast bowl in the sink. A newspaper lying on the sofa.

But the flat looked clean and serviceable. And silent. Lonely. It was very small. A sitting room and kitchen, divided by an island bench, and one other room, presumably the bedroom and en suite bathroom. Had she been lonely, living here all by herself? Had she missed him at all in the past two years? Or had she only missed…Damn it, of course she'd missed her baby. *Their* baby. They'd both lost a part of themselves when…Lily died. They'd lost their marriage. Lost each other. He heaved a sigh.

"Oh heck, sorry about the mess." Annabel started darting around, scooping up litter, rinsing crockery, putting things away, rearranging cushions on the sofa. There were a couple of leather armchairs flanking a low coffee table, an antique desk and a small bookshelf crammed with journals, textbooks and a few novels. No photographs on display. He couldn't even see a TV set. Maybe it was in her bedroom.

The thought of her bedroom stirred an aching hunger deep inside him. It had been far too long since he'd shared a bedroom with…his wife. She *was* still his wife. Did she ever think of him—her husband—with the same passion, the same burning need? He'd seen a hint of it—more than a hint—back in Venice, but at the first imperious summons from her law firm, she'd dropped him and run, intent only on rushing back to London. He wondered if she would tell him what was so urgent that they'd cut short her planned week of recovery in the Venice sun. Or would she just dismiss it as "work"?

"Please don't fuss," he said. "And there's no need for you to cook anything. I'll just make myself a sandwich. Got any bread?"

"No, you won't, after waiting all this time for me. You'll sit down in this armchair and put your feet up." She dragged up a stool for him. "While you're resting your poor aching bones, I'll change out of this suit and then make you an omelet."

She disappeared through a doorway, shutting the bedroom door behind her. He was tempted to go after her there and then, but he had something else to do while he had the chance. He burrowed into his backpack and pulled out the purchase he'd made earlier in the day. With it gripped in his hand, he slipped into the kitchen, deposited it where it belonged and returned to the lounge.

He was sprawled in the armchair with his feet up when she came back wearing a pale blue tracksuit, with comfortable slip-ons in place of her elegant black shoes. Easy to slip on, easy to slip off, he found himself thinking rather wildly.

"Still awake?" she asked as she veered into the

kitchen, the lower half of her body disappearing behind the island bench.

"Wide awake," he assured her with a roguish smile, aware of bristling nerve ends that would only need a touch or a look to burst into fire.

She looked up at that, caught his smile and broke the egg in her hand. Luckily, she was holding it over a bowl. He watched as she broke more eggs, heard rattles and clunks as she delved into drawers, and the clatter of plates. Vigorous whirring sounds followed, and in no time at all his omelet was cooked and ready, along with two slices of toast.

"No need to move." She reached him in a couple of strides and thrust a tray under his nose. "Coffee to follow?"

"That sounds great. Thanks. Mmm, this looks good." He virtually licked his lips, bemused at her efficiency in the kitchen. During their marriage they'd had a housekeeper to cook for them ninety percent of the time. He remembered the rare weekends at home when he'd barbecued and they'd sat at the outdoor table and actually talked and relaxed for a few hours instead of working.

If they ever got back together, he vowed, things were going to be different. He was going to make sure they spent more leisure time together, that she didn't burn herself out at work and get sick again, that they took more time to enjoy life.

It was still a big *if*.

The welcome aroma of coffee was already wafting from the kitchen. "You'll join me, I hope?" he said, wondering if she was feeling the same expectant buzz that was tingling through him. "After all those hours of work you must be ready to relax yourself."

"I never say no to a coffee."

She sounded more tense than tingly with longing, he thought. Was she wondering if he intended to stay in London or was just passing through on his way back to Australia? Wondering if he'd come to say goodbye, after giving up on her and deciding to call the whole thing off? Or was *she* about to call it all off? If it had ever really been on.

There was that damned *if* again.

"That was delicious," he said, swallowing his last mouthful. It had gone down in double-quick time. "No assistance from the hired help, either," he quipped. "I'm impressed." He grinned as he said it.

"I could do better than that if I put my mind to it," she declared loftily, grabbing his tray as he started to get up. "Coffee coming up." She was back in a couple of minutes with the same tray, bearing two steaming coffee mugs and some cookies. She put them down on the coffee table. "Help yourself."

He reached for a chocolate Tim Tam. His favorite. "Yum. You're spoiling me."

"With that puny meal? Bet it didn't even hit the sides." She ran glinting green eyes over him, reactivating those buzzing nerve ends.

"It was just right." *Down, boy!* He sank back in his chair. "Now, please, *you* sit down."

"Yes, master."

His skin prickled. She'd called him that sometimes during their marriage. *Early* in their marriage. It chuffed him to hear it again, because it was said in the same teasing way, not meaning a word of it. They'd always been an equal partnership, never master and slave. Never like her father and mother.

He watched her flop into the armchair opposite, heard her exhale deeply before she reached for her coffee. He pursed his lips, and frowned. "You think *I'm* half-asleep on my feet. Look at *you*."

"I'm fine. It's been a long day, that's all."

"Do you work this late every night?"

"I've been away from work for a while, remember. I have a lot to catch up on." As her gaze caught his, he saw something flash in her eyes—as if she wasn't telling him everything. He let it go—for now.

"You realize what you're doing to yourself, working such long hours. You've already been sick. You still look as if a strong wind would blow you away."

"So I lost some weight. It won't take long to stack it on again. I'm normally very fit and don't need much sleep. You know that. Drink up your coffee."

He took a sip, but couldn't resist a last word. "I thought you might have learned something from that bout of pneumonia. And from Venice…" He let that sink in for a moment. "That there's more to life than work. Everyone deserves some time off. Not just recovery time after an illness. Regular time off. Evenings and weekends, at least."

"You never used to take any time off," she reminded him. "You always worked longer hours than I did."

"Not any more. I've left all that behind, remember." He heard his voice harden and shivered, a shadow brushing over him. *Make a mistake in life and you pay the price…*

He felt her looking at him, and glanced up. Their gazes locked. The clear green of her eyes swam into the blue of his. He had the feeling she was looking right through him, into his darkest, most secret depths.

"But is your life as satisfying now?" she asked finally, her voice infinitely gentle, yet demanding the truth.

He stifled a pang. How to answer that? He knew how. "It will be if you're in it," he said. Damn it, he'd had it with pussyfooting around. He wanted her back. Their few days in Venice had proved that she wanted him, too, if not as much as her career. But he could live with that.

He saw her lips part, moist and enticing.

Annabel pressed a hand to her chest. He'd sidestepped her question, but his answer... Her heart fluttered wildly beneath her fingers. He wanted her back in his life? "I—I thought you might have come to say goodbye," she said weakly. "After the way I left you in Venice. I thought you might have been, uh, on your way back to Australia by now."

He pursed his lips. "Is that what you wanted?"

"No! Yes! Only—only if it brought you back to the work you love...neurosurgery. Where you *belong,* Simon," she stressed, rushing on before he could stop her. "Remember your vow to your mother? She would have been so proud of you, knowing you've saved so many people like her...people who needed the best. *You're* the best, Simon. Don't waste your talents. People with serious brain disease and injury *need* the best. They need *you.*"

He winced and shook his head. "I don't think so. I let you and our daughter down. I've let others down." His mouth looked suddenly pinched and pale. "I don't want to fail anyone again, have any more lives depending on me. Forget it, Annabel. Please."

He'd let others down? Well, of course…he must have, in such a dangerous, crucial field. No brain surgeon, no matter how talented, could save everybody. Some cases were beyond saving. Like…Lily.

"Simon, just listen to me," she pleaded. She couldn't let him go on torturing himself over Lily, trying to save her feelings by pretending she had nothing to do with it. "You never let me down. I let *you* down. If anyone's to blame for Lily's death, it was me. I didn't move quickly enough. I couldn't protect her from that speeding car. I've been racked with guilt ever since. It nearly killed me, knowing I let it happen right in front of me."

He groaned, shocked repudiation in his eyes. "*You've* been racked with guilt! Oh Bel, it was a hit-and-run, for God's sake. A stolen car that was traveling so fast it lost control at a pedestrian crossing. You wouldn't have had time to react or get out of the way. Nobody held you responsible."

"You—you never blamed me?"

"Look, I might have for an instant, when our daughter was brought into the hospital and I learned that her pram was hit when you were crossing a road. But once I heard what actually happened…no, never! *You* weren't to blame, Bel."

"I still felt it was my fault. I—I thought you did, too…all along. I didn't blame you for hating me and shutting me out." She looked down at the hands in her lap. "But it hurt me so much. You wouldn't talk to me, or discuss it. You couldn't even look at me. I—I couldn't live with it any more, the way you turned away from me. I thought our marriage was over. There seemed no point going on."

Another agonized groan rose from his throat. "You thought I hated *you*?" He stared at her in disbelief. "Oh Bel, I hated *myself*, blamed *myself*! With all my so-called skills, I wasn't able to save her. That's why I couldn't talk about it or look you in the eye. I thought you blamed me, too. I couldn't bear to look into your eyes and see the despair...the condemnation I thought I'd see there. It was even harder, knowing I deserved it."

"But you didn't deserve it!" she cried. "I never blamed you, Simon. Never! I was devastated when you couldn't save Lily's life—it made me feel even more guilty—but the doctors told me that nothing you did could have saved her. Nobody could have saved her. You've nothing to blame yourself for!"

He seemed to physically reject that, his shoulders slumping. "Haven't I? You don't know the half of it." His voice was so low she could barely hear the words.

"What do you mean?" Her own voice was a breathy whisper.

He straightened his shoulders and gave a slow shake of his head, reaching out to put his empty coffee mug down on the table. "We seem to have deviated from where we were." His tone had changed. It was velvety smooth now, almost a caress. "We were talking about us...our future...not the past."

Our future. Her heart lifted. That was what mattered,

not regrets, or breast-beating, or mulling over past traumas that nobody could have foreseen or prevented.

"Is that why you followed me here to London, instead of wiping your hands of me—as I expected, after the way I rushed off and left you?" Her eyes sought his. "You wanted to talk about…our future?"

He cocked a dark eyebrow. "I wasn't going to give up on you without finding out *why* you left Venice in such a hurry. Are you going to tell me what was so important you had to drop everything and run? Or were they simply missing you at work and felt they couldn't manage any longer without you?"

She smiled. "No…it was a bit more than that." She could hardly hold it back now. But tempted as she was to blurt it out, she forced herself to slow down, to pick her words. Hoping that what she had to tell him would make him happy.

"They told me that Guy Mallaby was coming to London, just for the day. He'd asked to see me."

"Mmm…the great Mallaby himself, eh? Royal command."

She searched his face. He was starting to suspect what was coming. She could see it in his eyes. A knowing glint in the heart-stopping blue.

"He's transferring me back to Sydney," she said, still holding back the important bit, letting this part sink in first.

"You're coming back to Sydney?" He hadn't expected that. But she could see it was welcome news to him, by the way his face relaxed and his blue eyes gleamed even more brightly. "When?"

"In two days. If I can be ready by then." She took a deep breath, and let it whoosh out again, clamping her mouth shut. On an impulse, she decided to hold back the news about Mallaby's offer of a partnership until she knew more about *his* plans.

Once Simon knew that her commitment to her law firm was going to be even more intense, possibly putting even greater demands on her, he might never go back to neurosurgery, fearing her new status could jeopardize their relationship. Once before, they'd both had equally demanding careers and they'd barely had time for each other, let alone for their child. If they were going to resurrect their marriage, she would want it to be a real marriage this time, a real relationship, with more sharing and togetherness, and the two of them spending more time with each other, doing different, relaxing things together, and maybe even...

She felt a tremor. Would Simon *want* another child? He still seemed to have some unresolved torment eating at him...some deeply buried anguish he still couldn't share with her. A trauma in his past, maybe, long before Lily.

Would she want another child herself? She hadn't wanted to think about it until now. It had been too painful to contemplate. But she realized she did...not yet, perhaps, but sometime, before it was too late. If Simon, in time, felt the same way.

She looked up at him. Best to take it one step at a time. And her first step, she decided, was to find out what *he* intended to do with his life.

Chapter Eight

Simon waited, wondering what was coming. He'd been watching her. She'd been chewing something over in her mind. He'd seen the wheels turning. Now she seemed to have come to some kind of resolution. He hoped he was going to like it.

"You said *coming back to Sydney*," she reminded him. "Does that mean you're on your way back to Sydney yourself?"

He relaxed. Was *that* what she'd been pondering so deeply? "I am now," he said easily. "If you'd been staying on in London, it would have depended on you. On whether you wanted me to stay."

"You would have stayed here in London, with me?"

"Sure. You need someone to keep an eye on you, make sure you're looking after yourself and eating properly, relaxing occasionally. Maybe you might even

decide you want your husband back…permanently."
His eyes danced, but there was an intensity in the blue.

"Simon, I—"

"I'm not asking for an answer now," he said, keeping his voice smooth. *Not feeling so smooth inside.*
"I'm just saying I'll be there for you. Here…or back in
Sydney, if that's where you're heading. You'll have time
to ease off and enjoy life a bit more if I'm there to take
some of the load off your shoulders. You can keep your
mind on your work and not get stressed and end up getting sick again, or burned-out. I'll have more time for
all that now that I'm not burning the candle at both
ends myself."

She didn't seem overjoyed about that. "I don't need
you to play nursemaid to me, Simon! You'll need to find
work yourself. The kind of work you've always wanted
to do and where you're most needed. It'll be easier back
in Sydney. You'll have every hospital clamoring for you
to work for them."

He sighed. "I've told you, Bel. I'm not going back
to neurosurgery."

Her eyes wavered under his, limpid green pools that
made him want to grab her and promise her anything.
Anything but that.

"Then work as a neurologist, like you did before, so
you're not wasting your talents."

"I didn't find neurology satisfying enough, challenging enough," he said. "I gave it away after a few months.
As soon as my hand was better." Only surgery had given
him that special buzz, that sense of fulfillment. But the
price was too great. His hands had taken enough lives
already. Worse, lives of loved ones close to him.

"You didn't find it satisfying because your heart's in surgery!" she cried, triumph glinting in her eyes. "Neurology's too close to neurosurgery, too much of a reminder of where your real talents and passions lie."

He heaved a deep sigh. "Annabel, I know you mean well, but forget it. I've lost the heart for it." He had to give her a better reason than that, had to convince her, make her believe him. "It destroyed us before, remember. Both of us working our butts off, clawing our way to the top of our respective fields, not leaving time for anything else. Or anyone else."

He stared into his coffee, thinking of the baby daughter he'd loved and lost, that they'd both loved and lost, and remembering how they'd thrown themselves even deeper into their work in their last few months together. To escape…forget…blot out what had happened…and other memories that didn't bear thinking about. When they'd needed each other the most, they'd turned away from each other, each nursing their guilty hang-ups instead of talking about them, instead of sharing their pain, grieving together.

He was still nursing hang-ups, damn it. And he still couldn't talk about…that other part of his life.

A swarthy face contorted with rage—a despised specter he'd managed to block from his memory for most of his life—flashed into his mind like an avenging devil. He savagely stifled it. If she knew… No! It was too early to lay stuff like that on her. He couldn't risk seeing her turn away from him again. Their relationship was still too fragile.

"We both screwed up," she agreed finally, and he heard the tremor in her voice, as if she'd been having similar thoughts about their driven careers and the heedless way they'd put their work ahead of everything else, even their baby daughter. "But it'll be different now," she insisted. "We know what it did to us. We won't let our careers rule our lives any more. Besides, we won't *need* to work at such a frantic pace, never taking any time off, driving ourselves into the ground. We've both…pretty well achieved our goals."

A spark lit up her eyes for a second, before it flickered away, her expression clouding. "But you're throwing your career away," she said sadly. "I never thought—" She broke off with a sigh. "Sorry, I know you've made up your mind. Have you thought about what you *do* want to do?"

"I've given it a bit of thought…yeah. Just a minute." He put down his coffee mug and stood up, holding out his hand. He couldn't stand it any longer. Having her at arm's length. Not touching her, or holding her, or feeling her warmth. Whatever he had to say to her, and whatever she had to say to him—because there *was* something, and he had a feeling he knew what it was going to be—he wanted her close, not on the other side of the room.

"Come and join me on the sofa," he invited, tugging her across the small space that had separated them.

He drew her down onto the cushions, still clasping her hand. Just the touch of her arm and shoulder against his, the tingling warmth of being so close, her teasing scent, aroused other emotions…more earthy emotions. He had to physically restrain himself from scooping her into his arms and carrying her into the bedroom then and there.

* * *

Annabel felt the physical impact of him as he leaned into her, her pulses leaping, skin tingling at the intimate contact. Was the same excitement coursing through *his* veins? He wasn't looking at her. There was a knot of tension in his jaw. Surely if he felt what *she* was feeling, he'd be making eye contact...wouldn't he?

Her hand trembled in his. *I've given it a bit of thought,* he'd said. Was he about to tell her something so unwelcome that he needed to hold her hand and have her close enough to comfort her?

"Whatever you decide will be all right with me," she said stoutly, though her voice wobbled a little.

He turned to her then, swallowing her with his eyes, a golden fire kindling in the blue depths for a second before he blinked it away. "Ah...yes...thanks." He seemed oddly discomforted. It made her realize suddenly that he hadn't been avoiding her eye so much as trying to control himself. A thrill ran through her at the thought.

She was almost disappointed that he *had* regained control.

"I've been toying with the idea of going into research," he said, absently fiddling with her hand. "If I can find a neuroscience research unit that's prepared to use my expertise. There's a lot being done in that area now...a lot that needs to be done."

Neuroscience research... She mulled it over for a second. He'd be making use of his expert skills, doing valuable work in the field he was trained in. But...

She flicked her tongue over her lips. "That sounds really worthwhile, vital work, Simon, and you'd be great at it. But…you're a surgeon, not a scientist. You wouldn't be hands-on, in direct contact with patients. And you're so good with people, with healing the whole person. Using your hands, and your exceptional skills and knowledge."

He looked ready to object at that, but she hastened on before he could. "You've never been a coldhearted, uninvolved type of specialist who treats his patients like objects rather than human beings. You care for your patients, follow up their cases, take a genuine interest in them, even become lifelong friends to some. Your humanity's legendary. It's part of who you are."

She could feel the tension in him. After a moment's pause, he said heavily, "Maybe I need to distance myself more. I tend to get too involved."

He was thinking of Lily. How he'd suffered after not being able to save her. But it wasn't his fault! Their poor darling had already been lost to them. Why couldn't he face up to that painful fact and let himself off the hook? With his expert knowledge, he must have known it was hopeless.

"Yes…caring about people hurts," she agreed, her voice husky. "But *not* caring makes you less of a human being, less of a doctor." She flushed. "Oh, Simon, I'm sorry!" She squeezed the hand holding hers. "You'll do a wonderful job in research. You'll be saving lives in a different way…by improving knowledge and finding new ways to deal with brain disease. Whatever you decide to do, I'll be behind you one hundred percent."

His eyes lifted. "Thank you," he said and brought up her hand, pressing it to his lips. "When we get back to Sydney I'll make some inquiries, find out which hospi-

tals have a research unit, and take it from there. Now…"
He put an arm round her and pulled her closer, peering
into her face. "You have something to tell *me*."

She looked up at him wonderingly. "Well, yes, I
have." Her chest heaved, her eyes suddenly glowing. No
point any more in *not* telling him. They would both be
back in Sydney soon…together, she hoped. Oh, how she
hoped!

"And it's the reason your office summoned you back
so urgently?" he probed gently. His eyes were encouraging, and so intensely blue she had the feeling they
were reading her mind, piercing her soul. "So that Guy
Mallaby could tell you in person?"

He's guessed, she thought shakily. He knows what's
coming. But was he going to be truly happy about it?
Their lives had changed so much. His life especially.
She swallowed and nodded. "Guy's offered me a partnership…back in Sydney."

To her delight his eyes flared in delight, the brilliant
blue dazzling her. "A partner! So…you've made it, Bel.
Congratulations!"

He caught her face between his hands and kissed her
on the lips, a quick hard kiss that he ended so abruptly
she almost groaned aloud, her lips aching to respond, tingling from the brief contact. Couldn't he sense that she
was longing for more? Her eyelashes fluttered upward.

"Stay right here, I'll be back." She was left staring
up at him as he pulled away and jumped to his feet.
"This calls for a celebration. Got any champagne
glasses?"

She relaxed, a bemused smile quivering on her lips.
"Only wine glasses, in the glass cabinet above the

bench. But I've no champagne. Not even a bottle of wine. Only mineral water. Sorry."

"Don't worry, I came prepared." He headed straight for her refrigerator.

She gave an uncertain laugh. "I would have noticed if there was a wine bottle in my fridge," she called after him. She'd gone to the fridge to fetch milk earlier.

"It's not in the fridge. I put it in the freezer to chill for a bit." She heard the clunk of a bottle landing on the bench and the clink of glasses.

He breezed back in with a bottle of Möet champagne and two wine glasses. With a flourish he removed the cork, which came out with a loud pop. He tilted the bottle, poured two glasses and handed her one.

"To my brilliant wife," he said as they clinked glasses.

Wife! He was already thinking of her as his wife again. She gulped. If only… *Oh dear God, if only!*

"I couldn't be more proud," he said, smiling his beautiful smile, "or more delighted for you."

For *her.* But what about himself? Would *he* be happy going into neuroscience research rather than being a hands-on neurosurgeon, making use of his brilliant skills?

"Thank you," she said, and took a sip, wrinkling her nose as the bubbles tickled her nostrils. "Very nice," she said, taking another sip. A glass of bubbly was just what she needed after her long roller-coaster day. "And very cunning of you, sneaking it into my freezer while I was out of the room. But what made you think we'd be celebrating?" She wondered if they should be celebrating at all, or if it was too soon, tempting fate.

"Just hoping. Call it intuition." Twinkling blue sparks danced in his eyes. "I figured...why else would they have recalled you from Venice so urgently?"

She gave a rueful shrug. "Any number of reasons. *I* thought I was about to get the chop."

"The chop! *You?*" He gave a booming laugh. "You're kidding. You've always been their golden girl. No one could have given more to the firm, worked harder, produced better results."

She sighed. "Not so much lately. I'd slacked off. Fallen ill. Taken time off. And then convalesced in Venice." And been sunk in misery before that, missing Lily, missing Simon, wallowing in pain and guilt. She'd only worked so hard to forget.

"Well, it obviously didn't spoil your chances," Simon drawled, his eyes soft and warm, filling *her* with warmth. He *is* genuinely happy for me, she thought, gulping. He's so different from my family. My father and brothers. She dropped her gaze to take another sip of champagne. Even her mother felt she was missing out on what really mattered...a home, a family...especially after losing her baby granddaughter.

"Sometimes I wonder if it's all worth it," she said, her tone pensive.

She could feel his eyes on her. "It's what you've always wanted, Bel, what you've worked so hard for. You deserve it. Now maybe you can ease off a bit...take time to smell the roses and enjoy your new standing in the firm."

Ease off? As partner, would that be possible? It was more likely she'd have greater responsibilities now, even more demands on her. She forced a smile, hiding her qualms. "I…don't think I've taken it in properly yet," she mumbled, and bit her lip.

The suspicion was growing that Simon was avoiding going back to neurosurgery, with its pressures and long hours, because he feared they might grow apart again and end up breaking up a second time. How could she bear it if he was refusing to go back so that he would have more time to make *her* life easier, taking on the bulk of the workload at home so that *she* could concentrate on *her* job?

"Come on, drink up," he urged, dashing more champagne into her glass. "You're just feeling nervous about what lies ahead, now that you've broken through the mythical glass ceiling and joined the big boys at the top. You've no need to be. You'll make a wonderful partner. The best ever. And I'll be right behind you." He paused, before adding softly, "If you want me to be."

"Oh, Simon, I don't want you *behind* me, I want you *with* me!" she cried, sure about that at least. "Alongside me as an equal partner, doing what makes you happy." She looked up at the man she adored and got lost in those mesmerizing blue eyes.

His face swayed closer, his eyes smoldering under her shimmering gaze. The touch and gentle pressure of his lips sent hot fire streaking through her. Her limbs were dissolving, the way they had four years ago on the night that had changed their lives, though they hadn't known it at the time.

"How about we finish our champagne in the bedroom?" His voice had dropped to a silky purr. "Champagne in bed sounds very sexy…"

Bed! She gulped, a deep longing welling inside her.

It had been so long. So longed *for*. She looked up at him with dazed eyes, suddenly feeling as nervous as a new bride. "I—I think I've had enough. I don't want to be tipsy when I go to work in the morning." Oh, brilliant, she groaned silently, why did I have to mention work? He'll think I'm still obsessed, that work's all I think about, and it isn't. I'm not. I'm only obsessed with *him*.

"You're right, it's a work night." Did his eyes flicker for a second? He took the glass from her hand and put it down on the table, placing his own beside it. "Besides, all we need…is each other." He pulled her to her feet and swung her up into his arms, as easily as if she were a child. Even knowing she'd lost weight, she marveled at his strength, the muscular power of his cradling arms, his firm, steady stride as he carried her across the room to the bedroom.

As he eased her through the open doorway, she had the heady feeling they were crossing the threshold into a new life together. *Were* they? Or was this simply an overwhelming rush of libido, the pent-up needs and emotions of the past two years demanding immediate release, fueled by the effects of the champagne?

Right at this moment, she didn't care. She only wanted one thing…*him*.

Simon was aware of the symbolic gesture in crossing the threshold and had his own hopes, his own questions, but they could wait. His longing to have his wife clinging to him again, melting inside him again, couldn't.

He lowered her down on the bed, wondering how he was going to be able to hold back, to control himself, before he thrust inside her as he ached to do. He must take his time, give *her* time, or it would be over so quickly she would end up disappointed...and maybe question his motives. He wanted her back in his life, not just in his bed.

"Don't sit up...don't move..." He slid in beside her, leaning on one elbow, looking down at her with hungry eyes. Her hair was spread over the pillow...not as it used to be when it was longer, a mass of tumbling waves, but still as lushly beautiful, still as richly vibrant, with its reddish sheen and golden highlights. It still made his hands itch to run through it.

He fingered the silken strands tentatively. "You have beautiful hair," he murmured, controlling other urges, gut-piercing urges, with an effort.

"But you prefer it long," she reminded him, and the huskiness in her voice was almost his undoing.

"I love it just the way it is. And I love you...just the way you are." *There, he'd said it.* He ran hot eyes down her slender body. And had to stifle a groan. "Let's get rid of these clothes." He ripped his shirt over his head without undoing the buttons, kicked off his shoes and wriggled out of his jeans, leaving only his skintight briefs that did little to hide the jutting arousal beneath. He saw her eyes riveted to his groin and felt himself harden even more.

"Now your turn," he growled, using fumbling fingers to help her pull off her sweatshirt and pants. She wore no bra or panties underneath. His mouth suddenly went dry. Her breasts seemed fuller, more sexy than he remembered, perhaps because her body was slimmer. He stroked a hand over one creamy breast and her nipple firmed at his touch. His insides wrenched.

"You're more beautiful than ever," he muttered through his teeth, hardly able to bear the sight of her smooth ivory body without ravishing it there and then. He'd never felt so aroused, so close to losing control. But he mustn't...not yet. He shifted his eyes to her mouth. *Start there...kiss her senseless...a kiss to end all kisses...until she wants you as much as you want her.*

But she had ideas of her own. In a provocatively languorous movement, she reached out and touched him. He arched back with an animal cry as a white-hot fire swept his groin.

"God, Bel, if you think I can wait now...!"

"I don't want you to wait!" she gasped, tugging at the band of his briefs with frantic fingers. "You'd better get rid of these..."

"I'll do it!" He tore them off, and then jerked back with a groan. "Oh hell, I nearly forgot. Just a minute..." She wouldn't want another unplanned pregnancy, any more than he would...especially now, with a promotion on offer.

She caught his arm. "You don't need to worry. I'm still on the Pill." It came out in tiny, breathless gasps.

She was? He looked down at her, remembering that she'd started taking the Pill after Lily was born. But they'd been apart for nearly two years...

"There's never been anyone but you, Simon," she assured him, gripping him more tightly. "I...I guess I was hoping you'd come and find me one day."

He felt a rush of love for her...and relief. "I've never wanted anyone else, either. God, if you knew how much I want you *now!*" A raging heat was roaring in his ears, passion rising like the hottest fire, clouding his brain.

"I want you, too! Oh *please,* Simon!" She moaned the impassioned plea, her fingers clawing at his bare skin. "I can't wait any longer!"

"Me, either!" With an agonized growl, he sank down on top of her, his fevered skin burning into hers, before he thrust into her in a frenzied merging of heat and dampness and raging, unstoppable need.

Annabel fell back onto the pillows with a rapturous moan. How could anything so quickly over, so explosively uncontrolled, have been so earth-shatteringly sublime, so unbelievably blissful, a thousand times more intense, more satisfying than anything they'd shared before? They'd both climaxed together, soaring to the heights with no seductive foreplay, no preliminary kissing or caressing, leaping straight into a raw animal coupling that wasn't to be denied.

Yet it had transcended all their previous times.

"Bel, I'm sorry," Simon muttered in her ear, through the damp strands that covered it. "I swore I wasn't going to rush you...that you were going to savor every delicious minute...every touch...until you were screaming for mercy, screaming for release."

She laughed softly. "I was screaming for release from the very first second you touched me. Couldn't you tell? I could no more wait than you could. I've missed you so much!"

He buried his face in the warm hollow of her throat. "If you knew how I've longed to hear that! I've missed you, too...so much I nearly went crazy. But for a long time..." He trailed off, his voice muffled.

"Go on, darling." The endearment she hadn't used for so long slid easily from her lips. "Tell me."

"I thought our marriage was finished, that I'd made you despise me and regret ever getting married in the first place." As she started to protest, he put a finger to her lips. "I wanted to go after you but... I couldn't. Not just because I'd wrecked my hand, after crashing it into that brick wall—a crazy thing to do, but I didn't care at the time—but because I was all locked up inside, sunk in a black pit—wallowing in...I don't know...grief, guilt, anger, defeat, dented pride—that stopped me from crawling back to you, begging forgiveness."

"Well, dearest, you know now...there was no need...there never was." She ran a loving hand over his thick wavy hair. "I blamed myself, not you. I thought *you*—"

"Bel, I'm sorry...I should have seen what I was doing to you. When I couldn't look at you or talk about it, I wasn't blaming you. I just felt so...beaten...as if I'd let you down, let Lily down. *I* felt responsible...even knowing deep down there was no hope for her."

An acknowledgment at last!

"What blind fools we've both been!" she said with a misty-eyed smile. And yet—she stifled a sigh—a part of him was still locked up, still haunted by *something*. And he still seemed unable to face whatever it was, let alone talk about it. And she didn't intend to spoil this magic moment by probing, dragging up demons that might fracture the fragile bonding between them. Maybe—hopefully—not so fragile after tonight.

Whatever his dark secret was, it would have to come from him...when he was ready.

She drew back a little to stroke his rough cheek with tender fingers, loving the sandpapery feel of him, and the fact that she could look into his eyes and see his love for her, *feel* it.

She still couldn't believe he was here with her.

"Thank heaven you did come after me," she whispered.

He caught her hand and pressed it to his lips. "I was missing you so damned much I couldn't stand it any longer. That cleansing year at sea, and the memory of you in my arms, helped to pull me out of the hole I'd fallen into and make me strong enough to come looking for you…and risk being rejected again."

"Hush. You know now how wrong you were, that I left because I thought *you'd* spurned *me.* We were both too wrapped up in our own guilt and remorse, blinded with grief and self-pity. We *both* felt we'd let down Lily, not only because of the…the accident, but for not giving her enough of our time. We've never grieved properly," she said pensively. "Never talked about her. About the joy she brought us. The beautiful memories she left us. The good times."

She held her breath for a moment, until he said softly, "You're right. We should remember her, celebrate her life, not try to forget her. She's still here in our hearts. And always will be." He pulled her back into his arms. "But tonight, my dearest one…tonight we're celebrating, remember. You're going to be a partner…and you and I are back together…for good this time. We *are*… aren't we?"

"Oh, Simon, yes!" Whatever they had yet to work out, or to work through, they would do it together. "I do love you so much."

"I love you, too. So much, it scares me."

She felt a faint qualm. He felt things so intensely. Whatever it was in his past that was still affecting him, it had colored his whole life, she suspected, intensifying his feelings for her, for Lily, for his patients. It made her wonder if Lily's death wasn't the only reason he'd given up neurosurgery.

"I'll never leave you again, Simon," she vowed in a low voice. "We'll make it work this time. I promise."

He gave her a quick squeeze, as if he felt too much emotion to speak for a second. When he finally did, his voice was a hoarse, wolfish growl. "You and I have a lot of time to make up…and we're going to start right here and now." He cupped her face with his hands and kissed her on the lips, the gentlest of kisses. "And this time we're not going to rush it…"

He kissed her again, then again, light brushes of his lips, applying a bit more pressure with each touch, his warm mouth finally opening over hers, moving slowly at first, tantalizingly…tasting, savoring, lingering, his tongue flicking and sliding over hers, making her heart rate quicken, before he deepened it into the longest, headiest kiss she could have dreamed of.

His hands were moving over her rapidly heating body, teasing her, circling her breasts, stroking her stomach, sending shivers of delight through her. She grabbed his hand and pressed it to the throbbing swell of her breast, wanting a more intimate touch. She felt her nipple tingle and tauten as his fingers pinched and rubbed the rosy peak until she was moaning and arching beneath him, silently begging for more. Mmm… such sweet torture!

With a muffled sound, he moved his hand away from

her breast and replaced it with his mouth, sucking at the sensitive nub until she was panting, her moist, burning body writhing beneath him.

He stopped suddenly, breathing hard, and lifted his head. "Hang on…let's slow things down…you're driving me over the edge again!"

"I don't care," she moaned.

"I do. I want to taste and feel every part of you this time, bit by tormenting bit, and I want it to excite you so much you'll be screaming for more…just lie back and enjoy…" He nuzzled his lips into her hair and flicked his tongue over her earlobe, sending erotic shivers through her. She whispered softly, relishing the delicious sensation.

He found her lips again and kissed her deeply, at the same time stroking his hand down her throat, over her taut breasts, down her stomach to the aching mound between her legs. What he did there had her arching frantically, moaning at the melting fire inside her, wanting more, demanding more. Her straining hips rose up, begging to have his body pressing against hers, on top of her, inside her, deep inside, but he was intent on tormenting her, keeping her waiting as long as he could, letting her squirm and whimper under the seductive thrust of his fingers.

She could feel his tension, his wire-tight control, and it drove her even wilder. When he finally brought his heated body down on hers and lunged inside her, they both rocketed out of control at the first powerful thrust, crying out as the sensations intensified and exploded, flooding them with a raging heat. Gust after gust of ecstatic sensation shook through them, a mindless passion sweeping them along, higher, and higher, until they hurtled over the edge together.

Chapter Nine

They both slept until morning, cradled in each other's arms. Simon woke first and lay for a while watching her, hardly able to believe she'd come to him so readily, given herself so completely, with so much still to be resolved between them.

She lay facing him, her golden eyelashes fanning her cheeks, her short silky hair a wild tangle round her face. He smiled as he looked down at her. He'd almost forgotten how she always slept with a hand curled under her cheek. It made her look so vulnerable, so trusting, almost childlike. For someone so competent and independent, so in control of her life, it was an endearing habit, making him feel fiercely protective, filled with love for her and determined never to hurt her again.

A shadow darkened his musings. The pain he'd inflicted on her wasn't the first time he'd hurt someone close to him, and the thought of it happening again was an abiding fear that seldom left him. He wondered if she would understand, and forgive him, if he told her. If he *could* tell her. He'd never spoken about it to a living soul. He'd tried to block it from his memory, but Lily's accident and his grinding sense of failure had brought the tormenting images back.

She opened her eyes and saw him staring at her. "Simon…what's wrong?" she whispered, as if she'd seen something in the depths of his eyes. Something that disturbed her.

"Nothing's wrong," he assured her, chasing away the shadows with a smile, his expression softening. He wanted nothing disturbing her at this point in time. Just when their lives were getting back on track. Just when she'd reached the shining pinnacle of her career and achieved her life's ambition. Just when she was about to move back to Sydney and take on challenging new demands and responsibilities.

Best of all, she seemed ready to settle back into married life…with him, if she meant what she'd said last night in the throes of passion.

"I was just thinking how precious you are to me," he murmured, brushing fine strands of hair from her eyes, "and how much I've missed you…and longed for you."

Her lovely green eyes turned misty. "Ditto," she said huskily, as if she couldn't trust herself to say more.

"You're agreeing to give our marriage another try?" he asked, just to make sure.

She pursed her lips. "Just a try?" she teased. "You think it's going to be so hard we might not make it?"

"Not from my side. I just want to be sure it's what *you* want."

"It *is* what I want. More than anything in the world." She reached up to rest a warm palm on his unshaven cheek.

More than anything? He felt his throat constrict. It was the first time she'd put him in first place, ahead of her career. Was it because she'd finally achieved the prize she'd been aiming for, the coveted partnership she'd craved for so long?

It didn't matter what her reason was. She wanted him back in her life. And he damned well wasn't going to let her get away from him again!

"Have you let your parents know you'll be coming back to Australia?" he asked, to defuse the emotion swirling between them. It was time to be practical, to make plans. "And told them about your partnership offer?" He knew how much it meant to her to be successful in her parents' eyes, to show them she'd reached the top, that she'd made it in a male-dominated world.

He saw something flicker in her eyes. "Not yet. I haven't had a chance. You, uh, rather took my mind off anything else."

He looked suitably chastened. Or pretended to. "Sorry. You probably planned to do all sorts of things last night."

"Not after working for so long and getting home so late. But I'll have to do my packing tonight, and some cleaning and other things. I'll call my parents then. That's if…you give me the chance." She gave him a provocative look that stirred up renewed heat in the pit of his stomach.

He quenched it—reluctantly. It wouldn't help things to make her late for work. "Do you have much packing to do?" He glanced round. And caught sight of a photograph on her bedside table. It was a family photograph of the three of them... Annabel, himself and Lily on the occasion of their daughter's first birthday. Her first and last.

He felt his breath catch as he released it. It must have been damned hard for her to look at that photo day after day, but she'd kept it beside her all this time, through all the pain and grief and hurt. He'd hidden away any photographs of his own, storing them with the few other possessions he'd kept in a facility in Sydney.

"Not much packing at all," she said. "It won't take me long to bundle up what I've accumulated. A furniture removals guy is coming in to help me and send it off." She followed the direction of his gaze, which he hadn't been able to pluck away from the photograph.

"That was a happy day," she said, her voice a trifle unsteady. "One of the happy memories we must cherish. We have a lot of wonderful memories of Lily, Simon."

"Yes, I know." He brought his gaze back to her face, relieved that he could finally talk about his daughter, and look at his wife when he did. "I kept her photos, too, but I put them into storage in Sydney when I sold the house."

"You sold your house in Paddington?"

He noted her use of the word *your,* not *our,* though they'd lived there together from the day they'd married. He'd bought the trendy terrace house when he sold his mother's house in Melbourne and moved to Sydney to specialize, renting it out while he was working in New York. He and Annabel had intended to buy a proper family home with a more spacious garden when Lily was older.

The darkness swirled back for a second, but he controlled it and answered in a reasonably steady voice.

"Yes. It seemed best, since I was going to be at sea for a year." Too many painful memories was the truth of it. His child...his wife... "So...where are we going to live when we get back to Sydney? You'd prefer an apartment in the city, close to your office?"

She seemed to hesitate. "I...guess so," she said finally. "It would be handy for you, too. I guess most research units would be at the big city hospitals?" She barely waited for a nod from him before adding, "But we won't have to rush into anything. Mallaby's are putting me into a city apartment for three months, to give me time to look around. It's close to Mallaby's, on the North Shore."

She looked up at him, a flicker of uncertainty in her eyes. "I'll let Guy know we're back together, and that you'll be moving in with me. You will, won't you?"

Was she afraid he might balk at moving into a Mallaby-owned apartment, even temporarily? "If we're back together, Bel, we live together," he assured her.

Her face relaxed. "Once we're back in Sydney, we can start looking for a more permanent place of our own."

He wondered if she would want a city apartment or a house with a garden. They'd had a child to think of before, but it would be just the two of them this time, and a garden wouldn't be necessary. He felt a twinge of...

He breathed in deeply, swallowing a sudden thickening in his throat. It couldn't be regret. The thought of another child sent cold shivers through him. It scared him to death. And he couldn't imagine Annabel wanting any more children, especially now she was going to be a partner.

He rolled her over and kissed her on the lips. "I'll be making you late for work."

"Oh heck, yes, I must fly!" But she seemed reluctant to move away.

"And I mustn't distract you," he said firmly. "Now or…tonight." He let his eyes linger for a long tender moment on her lips and felt a wave of satisfaction when he saw her cheeks glow. He had to force himself to go on, to say what he'd made up his mind to tell her. "I think I should fly back ahead of you, if I can get a flight today, and check out a few things—my investments, banking, that sort of thing. I'll stay at a hotel until you join me."

For a second, he thought she was going to protest, her lip trembling in a way that made him want to grab her there and then and keep her in bed all day. But she drew back instead and nodded slowly, making him glad he hadn't weakened.

"That might be a good idea," she conceded, a faint sigh in her voice. "It'll give you a chance to make inquiries about openings in neuroscience research."

"Yeah…that, too."

"If you're sure that's what you want to do?" She was staring up at him with her clear green eyes, searching deep, showing such genuine caring for him, a caring he'd thought had gone forever, that the usual curt retort on his lips died.

"It is," he said gently, ignoring a faint niggle that stirred whenever the subject came up. "As you said, I'll still be using my training and expertise…which you must feel happy about."

"If research is going to make *you* happy, darling, then I'll be happy, too."

He sensed—being more attuned these days to every betraying nuance in her voice, every glimmer in her expressive green eyes—that she still wasn't sure he *would* be happy. He smiled, partly to reassure her and partly because it was the second time she'd called him *darling* since they'd met up again, and that *certainly* made him happy. A small thing, but it meant a lot to him.

She left him reluctantly, wondering if he'd still be there when she came home after work. He was on the phone to Qantas when she walked out the door. If he had no luck with them, he was going to try other airlines. She half hoped he wouldn't get a flight with any of them until tomorrow, but common sense told her that Simon was right—if he stayed on at her flat, they wouldn't be able to resist spending the entire evening making passionate love and she'd never get anything done.

And besides, a day or two in Sydney on his own, being around his old medical and neurological cronies, sniffing out jobs in neuroscience research, just might make him think again about what he *really* wanted to do—especially if his medical colleagues wanted him back in neurosurgery, where he'd made such a name for himself. With her not there to distract him and maybe stiffen his resolve, he just might be persuaded…

She was convinced his heart still lay in neurosurgery, if only he could shake off the shadows that still seemed to haunt him…and stop thinking of *her,* putting *her* needs before his.

He'd promised to keep in touch by cell phone, but she'd warned him she mightn't have her phone switched on all day. Cell phones were frowned on at meetings and during work-related discussions, which were bound to snowball with her leaving London in two days.

"You can always leave a message with my secretary Liz," she told him, hoping that wouldn't be necessary. The thought of him leaving without speaking to her himself made her spirits dip. "Just keep your own phone on, okay, so I can call you back?"

"I promise. If I have no luck with a flight today, I guess you'll find me still here when you get home tonight." His eyes danced wickedly, warning her what to expect if he was still around. "But just in case I do get a flight, here's something to remember me by…" And he'd given her a deep, knee-weakening kiss that she was never likely to forget, wrecking her freshly applied lipstick and leaving her heated and breathless, a kiss that she knew would haunt her dreams and leave her aching for more and longing to be back in his arms *soon.*

Simon dialled Annabel's cell phone number, hoping she wasn't at a meeting. He relaxed when he heard it ringing.

"Annabel Hansen." She was using her businesslike voice, yet his ears, sensitive to any undertone, picked up a faint questioning note.

"Yeah, it's me," he said. "Can you talk?"

There was the faintest pause. He could hear voices in the background. "Just for a second," she said, which, he gathered, meant, *Nothing too personal*.

"Right, I'll be quick. I have a flight at two o'clock, but with the delays at Heathrow, and the time it'll take to get there, I'll need to leave now."

"Oh. I was half hoping—" She didn't finish the thought.

"Yeah. Me, too." He dropped his voice. "It's killing me to leave you, Bel, but I'd just get in your way. You've a lot to do, and so do I. Just a couple of days, honey, and we'll be back together again. Just don't go having second thoughts."

"I won't!"

He hoped she meant it. "I'll call you when I get to Sydney. Or you can call me…anytime. I'll be there to pick you up at the airport in a couple of days."

"You don't need to do that. Guy Mallaby said he'd pick me up. He'll be back in Sydney by then."

"Ah." For the first time in his life, Simon felt a stab of what could only be jealousy. Which was dumb. Mallaby was at least fifty, and happily married as far as he knew. It just showed he wasn't sure of her yet. Or of his own place in her life. Whereas she…

She'd just achieved the cherished goal she'd worked so long and hard for and, happy as he was for her, determined as he was to make her new role easier, he found himself wondering if it was going to change her, consume her, and ultimately affect their marriage. Their still vulnerable marriage.

He would just have to make sure it didn't. Finding the right job, a satisfying job that would still allow him time to give her the support she was going to need, had to be his first priority. His funds wouldn't last forever, and there was no way he was going to sponge off his wife.

"Simon?"

"Sorry. Tell Guy there's no need for him to pick you up. Your husband will be there to meet you." The sooner her colleagues knew they were back together, the better. "You'd better go. Bye, darling. Love you."

"Uh, me, too," she said, sounding a bit distracted. He could hear a man's voice calling her name. "I...I'll speak to you later." He heard a click and she was gone.

He puffed out a sigh, wondering if he was making a mistake leaving her so soon after finding her. If she felt he was turning away from her again, shutting her out again...

Damn it, Pacino, you're being pathetic. I thought you'd finished with all that self-doubt and feeling sorry for yourself. She's given you a second chance...grab it.

He jammed his cell phone into his pocket and reached for his bag.

Annabel worked hard for the rest of the day, but she found it difficult to concentrate on what she was doing, on anything that was said to her, or on the many phone calls she had to make or deal with. There'd been something about Simon's call earlier, about the way he'd gone quiet when she'd mentioned Guy Mallaby's name, that kept niggling at her.

Was he secretly worried about her promotion, her new elevated status? Worried she'd have no time or place for him?

It *was* going to mean a big change in her life—partners had the ultimate responsibility for the integrity and financial success of the firm—and she was going to have to be careful it didn't jeopardize her relationship with Simon. He came first in her life...

She blinked a little, realizing it was the first time she'd consciously thought of him that way. Her high-powered career, her burning ambition to achieve a partnership to throw in her father's face and secure her place in a male-dominated world, had been so all-consuming that everything else in her life, every*one* else— her husband and her child, the two people she'd loved most in the world—had been largely pushed into second place. It was a sobering thought.

No matter what new responsibilities and challenges lay ahead of her, she mustn't let it happen again. She *wouldn't* let it happen again.

It was torture waiting for him to call. Not that she expected to hear from him yet. He'd be in the air for about twenty-three hours.

It was amazing how quickly and efficiently you could get things done when your mind was elsewhere. She barely noticed the cleaning and tidying and packing until it was virtually done. Having professional help, she soon had all her clothes and books and knick-knacks packed neatly away. The only things left were what she'd need the next day. She'd pack those into a suitcase and take them with her.

She made herself a cup of coffee and flopped down on the sofa, reaching for the phone. It would be around breakfast time in Sydney...a good time to catch her parents at home. Her heart began to pump a little faster as she dialed her old home number.

"Joe Hansen." The familiar gruff voice raised her hackles, as it always did. From experience, she knew she had to be on her toes with her father, always on the defensive, prepared for a fight.

"Hullo, Dad. It's Annabel. How are you and Mum?"

"Oh, you've remembered we exist, have you?"

"Didn't you get my postcard from Venice?" As the question left her lips she realized they couldn't possibly have received it yet. She'd only posted it a couple of days ago, and Italian mail was notoriously slow. Even so, her father's caustic question stung. He'd obviously forgotten the Christmas and birthday cards she'd sent them.

"So you're both well?" she said quickly, wishing her mother had answered the phone. Suddenly, the big news she'd wanted to gloat about to her father had turned to sawdust in her mouth.

"Your mother's had an operation on her feet. Bunions." His tone was more derisory than sympathetic. "She's lying in bed with her feet up," he grumbled. "Can't do a thing."

So his domestic slave wasn't able to run around after him. Annabel felt a malicious satisfaction. Her father was actually having to do something for his wife for a change? How she'd love to see that!

She asked in mock sympathy, "So you have to cook the meals and clean the house?" With the reluctant help of her lazy brothers, no doubt.

"Over my dead body," came the gruff reply. "Your Aunt Barbara's staying with us until your mother's back on her feet."

Annabel gave a shake of her head. He couldn't even look after the house or care for his ailing wife for a few *days?* Typical! "Well, lucky you," she said, her tone dry.

"What's this about Venice?" he snapped. "I thought you were still working in London?"

"That's why I'm calling. They're transferring me back to Sydney tomorrow. And—" she swallowed "—Simon and I are back together."

She hoped she wasn't being premature, tempting fate. They weren't actually living together *yet.* But they would be soon, she told herself fiercely, and this time they were going to make it work.

"Well, at least you're showing a bit of sense there," came her father's tart comment. "We could never understand why you left him in the first place. Your precious career, I suppose. Nothing else mattered to you. Even your own child didn't divert you from your course."

She nearly cried out, the pain was so acute. "My career had nothing to do with our separation," she finally managed to scrape out. Did her parents honestly believe that her career meant more to her than her beautiful baby daughter? She was conscious of a sudden searing heat in her cheeks. Could *she* honestly say that her career hadn't obsessed her to the point of pushing Lily into second place? How many times had she left her with a nanny? Or with Simon...on the rare occasions he was at home himself?

"That's all in the past now," she mumbled into the phone. She'd never given her father a reason for her marital breakup and she wasn't about to now. He'd never understand. He didn't have the empathy or the sensitivity to understand. "Can you put me onto Mum now?"

"Your mother's asleep. I'll tell her you called."

"I'll call again when I get to Sydney and see how she is. Better go now. I've still a lot to do."

"Hmph. Speak to you soon." The line went dead.

Annabel's mouth dipped. No endearments. No loving words. No softening. But that was her father. The world revolved around him, not around his family. Except when something they did affected him.

She realized she'd hung up without telling him she'd been offered a partnership—the one thing that might have impressed him, and made him see her career in a more worthwhile light. But somehow it didn't seem so important anymore. At that moment, it no longer mattered to her what her father thought of her or of the life she'd chosen.

It didn't even seem so important to *her.*

You're tired, she told herself. You've been working flat out all day and all evening and you need a darn good sleep.

And she was missing Simon. That was what it boiled down to. Once they were back together, and they were both settled back in Sydney, with Simon in a new and challenging job, and she with her own new challenges at Mallaby's, everything would look different, brighter, more positive.

Her father had had his usual dampening effect on her…that was all it was.

She went to bed and conjured up an image of Simon, gloriously naked and tanned, holding her close, kissing her until she was moaning for more, driving her wild with his seductive hands and his hard, heated body. And when she drifted into sleep, still thinking of the man she loved, still aching for him, all her lurid longings and fantasies came true in her wildly erotic dreams.

Chapter Ten

Annabel emerged from Sydney Customs pushing a trolley holding her suitcase and carry-on bag. She looked around, seeking the one face in the crowd she was anxious to see. She'd let Guy Mallaby know that she and Simon were back together and that her husband would be picking her up. Guy had sounded delighted, issuing an invitation for the coming weekend that included Simon.

Where *was* Simon? All she could see was a multitude of faces, bobbing shoulders and waving arms. Several international flights had arrived around the same time, and every friend and relative in Sydney seemed to have crowded into Arrivals to greet their loved ones.

And then she saw him, looming head and shoulders above an excitable family group crowded in front of him. His bronzed face was slashed with a smile. And in that instant, everyone around him melted away, and she had eyes only for him. She drank in the brilliant blue gaze under the dark arched eyebrows, the windblown black hair and broad shoulders, and felt her knees go weak.

Her husband...the love of her life...waiting to sweep her into his arms and into a new life together. Something she'd never dared to believe would happen, except in her fairy-tale dreams.

Was the fairy tale actually coming true? Would they be able to make their marriage work this time? She thought of the secret anguish Simon still hadn't revealed to her and resolutely dismissed it from her mind as she ran to him and fell into his arms. Whatever was tormenting him, it belonged in his past and had nothing to do with the two of them.

But she knew in her heart that whatever it was *did* affect both of them. Having secrets, refusing to share an agonizing inner hell, had torn them asunder before.

Simon had seen her expression change from anxiety to glowing relief when she saw him, to a series of less readable emotions as her beautiful green eyes had virtually swallowed him up.

He felt a tightness in his chest as she flung herself into his arms. She was still unsure of him—or of herself?—but she was obviously happy to see him, to be back with him, and that was all that mattered for now.

The feel of her wonderfully soft, responsive lips under his and her warm soft curves melting into him was all he could think about for the next few minutes. It was only when the crowd jostled them that he drew back and reached for her trolley.

"We're blocking the way. Grab my arm, Bel, and let's go. My car's in the carpark."

"You've bought a car already?"

"A secondhand one. A medical friend wanted to buy his wife a new car and get rid of her old one. It's small but it's zippy and in good nick. How was your flight?"

"Perfectly comfortable. I even managed to sleep. Mallaby's sent me back Business Class." He saw her flush, and wondered if she was embarrassed by that... embarrassed for *him,* because he was without a job and had flown back Economy.

A small smile tipped the edge of his mouth. She *thought* he was still without a job. She'd know soon enough.

Annabel drew in a shaky breath. She and Simon had always been equals in the past, with high-powered jobs and plenty of money coming in on both sides. As a partner, she would have even more money coming in. Would he mind if she was earning more than he was, providing more than he was, spending more hours working than he was?

She nibbled at her lip. He'd always been so self-sufficient and almost arrogantly self-reliant and confident, earning a packet as a top neurosurgeon, owning his own home, running an expensive car, always wanting to pay for any dinners or entertainment, though she'd eventually succeeded in changing his thinking there. She'd been just as independent and determined to share costs, not wanting to rely on any man, even the husband she loved. Her mother's experience with her father had taught her that.

"You want to head straight for your apartment?" Simon asked when they reached his car. A far more modest car than he'd been accustomed to driving, but what did that matter as long as it was reliable?

"Won't you want to pick up your own things first?" she asked. "Where's your hotel?"

"I've already checked out. My things are in the trunk, along with some groceries from the supermarket. I'll stop off at a 7-Eleven on our way and pick up milk and perishables. The stuff I left in storage a year ago can stay there till we find a permanent place."

Stuff? All his possessions, he meant.

"What about—" she began and had to stop, clear her throat, and start again. "What about Lily's things? Toys and—and baby clothes? Did you keep anything?" She held her breath, half expecting him to close up again and retreat from her as he had in the past. But he answered without a pause, looking straight at her.

"I called a charity and gave most of her things to them…except for some photographs and personal bits and pieces—a gold bracelet, a Bunnykins dish, her favorite teddy, things like that—that I thought you might like to have sometime." His eyes were sad rather than remote, showing emotion he'd previously kept firmly buried and locked away.

She smiled, her eyes misty with gratitude…and poignant memories. "Let's keep them in storage till we have our own place," she said, thinking pensively of the empty rooms they were going to have without children to fill them. Would her flourishing career compensate for that loss? Her arms suddenly felt empty, and she reached for him, wanting him to fill the aching void. "I'm glad we're back together," she said huskily.

He folded her in his arms, pressing her into a welcoming wall of solid muscle. "Me, too," he said fervently, and kissed her—only to break it off before it could get out of hand, muttering. "I can think of better places for this than an airport carpark."

"I agree," she said, her lips still tingling, wanting more. "Let's get going." She eyed him hungrily. "The agent's left a key for us in the letter box."

She gave him the address and they headed for the North Shore.

"Well, this won't be hard to take," Simon said as he followed her into the modern first-floor apartment that would be their home for the next three months—unless they found their own place before then. "Tasteful. Relaxing. Great view over the harbor. Central heating. And all mod cons, by the look of it." He carried their groceries into the shiny space-age kitchen and started piling things into the refrigerator and stacking the shelves. With her help, they soon had it all done.

"Yeah…I reckon we should be comfortable here," he repeated, "until we find our own place."

"You really like it here?" She was eyeing him anxiously, and he wondered if it was because her law firm was putting them up here, rather than her husband and so-called provider. He swung her round and looked her straight in the eye. Didn't she know by now that he was nothing like her father? That he was no sexist control freak who must have his woman dependent on him?

"I really like it," he said, letting his hands rotate gently over her shoulders, his palms bathing her with their warmth. "I'd be happy anywhere, so long as you're with me."

He felt her relax, saw her softly curved lips spread in a smile. "That goes for me, too. Uh, I hope it's going to be convenient to where you'll be working?" It was the closest she'd come to asking if he'd found a job.

"No problem. Just a short drive over the Harbor Bridge." He tried to sound enthusiastic. He damned well *was* enthusiastic. All those years of study and hard work, gaining skills and experience, weren't going to be wasted. Okay, apart from his hands-on, life-or-death, emotionally draining surgical expertise. And that he could do without.

"You've found a job already?" Her face brightened. "Tell me!"

Seeing the joyful anticipation lighting up her face made him remember her impassioned outburst, *I don't need a nursemaid,* and her insistence that, *We're equals, you and me.* His eyes prickled with his love for her. Happy as she was with her own promotion, she wanted him happy and fulfilled in his work, too. He wondered if he would be. And then kicked himself for having doubts.

"I've been offered a full-time consultancy at St. Hugo's Hospital in their new neuroscience research unit, starting the week after next. It's only for six months, but it'll be regular weekday hours and if I feel right doing research, I'll apply for a more permanent position after that. If not there, then somewhere else."

She seemed satisfied with that. "Good on you, darling. I knew you'd be snapped up the minute people knew you were back. You—you haven't been hassled to go back into surgery?"

He shrugged off the loaded question. "It's not an option. What about you, Bel?" he asked, changing tack. "When do you go back to work?"

"On Monday." She hesitated for a second, then said, "Guy Mallaby has invited us to his country house in the Blue Mountains for the weekend. All the partners and their wives and children are going. It's partly to welcome me back. To welcome *us* back," she amended, "and partly to celebrate Matt Dwyer's fortieth birthday. He's one of the partners."

"And to celebrate your new partnership?" He cocked an eyebrow, and smiled. "No need to be bashful about it, sweetheart. I'm really proud of you. And pleased for you."

Her eyes melted under his. "Thank you, darling, but celebrations would be a bit premature. I haven't actually signed on the dotted line yet. We have to discuss all that next week."

"Just formalities," he said dismissively. "Everyone at Mallaby's must know about your offer and will want to congratulate you. It's no secret, is it?"

"No, of course not. The partners had to be consulted. And agree to it."

"Which they obviously have." He dropped a kiss on the tip of her nose. "It's a triumph for you, Bel. A wonderful achievement. Mallaby's first woman partner. Enjoy it." He kissed her again, on the lips this time, and as a spurt of hungry desire spiraled through him, he groaned and wrenched his lips away. "I should let you sleep first…recover from your—"

Feverish hands gripped him. "I don't need sleep, I just need *you!*" Hot, passionate lips recaptured his, snatching the breath from his lungs, smothering further argument.

Argument was the very last thing on his mind.

Annabel dragged him to the bedroom, still wildly kissing him. Their hands were all over each other, ripping and pulling as they stumbled into the room, leaving items of clothing littering the floor in their path. By the time they reached the double bed, they were both naked and panting with their need for each other, their fiery bodies dewy with sweat.

"Don't leave me again!" she gasped out as they tumbled onto the soft mauve-and-blue duvet, still clinging to each other, emitting animal sounds that only inflamed them both further. "I've had erotic dreams of you every night!"

"Well, it's time to start putting those erotic dreams into practice, lady," he murmured, rolling her onto her back. "Your dream man's here now."

She shivered in languorous ecstasy as his hand slid across her sensitized belly, beginning a lust-arousing exploration of her soft flesh. When he reached her breasts, the sensitive peaks were already rock-hard, waiting for the sensual rub of his fingers, the tormenting touch of his lips and flashing tongue.

Her reaction was swift and violent, her body jerking upward. "Oh God, Simon!" A searing heat rushed into her lower body. "If you only knew what you…ohhh," she moaned, "no other man has ever…"

"I'd throttle any other man who tried," he growled,

his powerful body shuddering as she wriggled against him, provocatively inciting him. He shifted with a grunt of impatience, rearing over her, then lowering himself down on top of her, letting her feel him, hard and throbbing, pressing into her yielding curves, intensifying the sensations running riot inside her. "I'll never let you go again, Annabel, so don't even think about it."

She was barely able to think at all, capable only of a breathy laugh as she arched against him, chasing away any shadows that still lingered, any qualms about the future. Nothing could come between them now...she wouldn't let it.

"I want you so much!" she groaned and opened her legs to him, welcoming him into her heaving, exquisitely aching body.

"You want to start thinking about getting dressed and doing some unpacking?" Simon asked later...much later. Shadows were lengthening outside, and lights already twinkled on the harbor below.

"Mmm...not really." She stretched luxuriously. "But I s'pose we'll have to. If you were my father," she said with a wry smile, "you'd be demanding your dinner by now."

"Well, I'm not your father, or anything like him," he reminded her, brushing her tangled hair away from her flushed face. "As you very well know. We'll order a pizza. By the way, have you ever played golf?"

She blinked up at him. *Golf?* Where did that come from? "No," she said, her smile bemused now. "Have you?"

"No. Which means we'll both be starting on a level

pegging. Why don't we try it? Put Sundays aside to play golf."

Put Sundays aside... Her heart gave a flutter. It sounded... wonderful. She pictured them out on a golf course together, enjoying themselves, spending a whole carefree day together, just the two of them. They'd never played any regular sport together, had seldom spent a full day together, just relaxing. They'd never had the time. Never *made* the time.

"What a great idea," she said. "But I don't even know how to hold a golf club, let alone how to hit a ball."

"We'll have a few lessons first, then it's just practice. Trial and error. With your competitive instincts, and mine, we should have some fun, don't you think? We could start this weekend if you like. Spend a relaxing Sunday together. Golf in the morning, house hunting in the afternoon."

"That sounds... oh heck, we can't." She bit her lip. "We're going to the Blue Mountains this weekend, remember? We're due there tomorrow—Saturday—in the afternoon. We won't be back until late Sunday." She stole an uncertain glance up at him. Would he see it as her work, her career, already taking over their lives again, coming between them as it had before?

"I could make an excuse... plead jet lag," she suggested, wondering if her future partners would accept that or see it as their new female partner showing her disdain and arrogance already.

Simon shook his head, his eyes showing nothing but tenderness as he absently wound a lock of her hair round his little finger. "Your work comes first," he said gently. "Spending time with your colleagues... showing you're one of them...doing the right thing as a new partner."

"I...guess so." She felt a surge of warmth. No, he was nothing like her father. He was genuinely supportive, proud of her, happy for her. He was a real man, a real partner, not an insecure, sexist control freak who could be threatened by a woman's success. "At least you and I will be together," she said. Along with the partners and their families. *Work* colleagues. Not *alone* together...as he'd wanted to be.

It made her remember an accusation he'd thrown at her in the past. *You've always put your career before our marriage.* She'd vowed never to repeat that mistake. Yet here she was, doing it again.

"I'm looking forward to it." He smiled his sexy, lopsided smile. "There'll always be another Sunday." He kissed her and swung off the bed.

She ran uncertain eyes over his smooth, tanned body, feeling a faint coldness where he'd been lying against her. Did he truly want to go? Or was he just thinking of *her,* wanting to make *her* happy? Didn't his own happiness matter to him?

He turned and looked down at her. "Want to have a shower before we get dressed? It'll save time if we have one together." His eyes, intensely blue against his sun-bronzed face, gleamed with that wicked twinkle again.

She ran her tongue over her lips at the bone-melting image that sprang to mind. "It'll save water, too," she breathed. Maybe he was just trying to reassure her, but she wasn't going to turn down an alluring invitation like that.

* * *

It was well into the evening by the time they ordered their pizza. They'd only unpacked the barest essentials by the time it arrived. The rest, they decided, could wait until morning.

Simon saw the way his wife was picking at her food and struggling to keep her eyes open. Jet lag had finally caught up with her. "As soon as you've had enough, you're going to bed. To sleep," he said firmly.

"I should call my mother first and see how she is," she said, stifling a yawn.

"She's not well?"

"She's had an operation on her feet, to remove bunions. Don't laugh. It's very painful, apparently."

"I'm not laughing. Is she at home or in hospital?"

"She's home now. My aunt's looking after her. My father's no help—he wouldn't know where to begin. He wouldn't even try." Her brow lowered.

"Well, he must have been impressed when you told him about your partnership offer." Simon gave a slow grin. "Suitably chastened, was he? Finally ready to admit that he's proud of his brilliant daughter? I hope you made him squirm?"

"My father wouldn't know how to squirm, let alone back down," she said dryly. "Actually, I didn't get a chance to tell him. We just talked about my mother. It… didn't seem the time to gloat."

"Just like I said, you're too modest. Never mind, it's probably best to wait until it's a *fait accompli*. Knowing your father, he'll be more impressed when it's all signed and sealed."

"Maybe. Let's not talk about him." She gave another huge yawn. "Sorry. I'm fading fast."

"Maybe you should call your mother in the morning, after you've caught up on your sleep. You're nearly dropping off in your chair."

"Yeah…maybe you're right. My father works Saturday mornings. Only my aunt and my mother should be at home."

"Then come on, I'll put you to bed. I'll stay up a while longer. I want you to sleep."

"Spoilsport." But she yawned as she said it.

She slept like a log. When she woke, a wintry sun was streaming in through the sheer curtains and Simon was already up, busying himself in the kitchen. The aroma of fresh coffee was wafting into the bedroom. She slipped into scuffs, pulled on a sweatshirt and padded out to join him.

He handed her a glass of orange juice. A faint burning smell rose from the toaster on the bench.

"You look fresh as a daisy," he said, running his blue eyes over her in a way that set her nerve ends jumping.

Liar, she thought, loving him for it. "You look pretty good yourself," she said, lapping up the sight of him over the rim of her glass. The impact of his athletic physique in a loose knit sweater and tight blue jeans was heart-stopping. His tumbled dark hair begged for her fingers to rake through it. And his crooked smile was making her limbs feel weak.

"What time are we due at Mallaby's place in the Blue Mountains?" he asked, bringing her back to earth. *Duty calls,* she thought with a sigh, wondering if that was how Simon saw the weekend ahead.

"Around 2 p.m.," she said, reaching for a cereal

packet and tipping some muesli into a bowl. "Guy's planning a late afternoon barbecue, which will probably go on well into the evening, if his past hospitality's anything to go by. Sunday morning, he's organizing a bush walk, rain or shine, he says. He'll provide wet weather gear if it rains."

"Sounds as if he believes in toughening up his partners," Simon commented, biting into a slice of toast spread with Vegemite.

"I think it's more a camaraderie thing to him," she said with a rueful smile. "Keep the troops pulling together...rally the flag, rah rah." *But the troops in the past had all been males.* "They'll expect me to fall behind or drop out," she muttered, "being a mere woman."

"But you'll make sure you outdo them all," came the knowing retort. "Even if it kills you."

She swallowed. He was right. She'd always put in extra time and effort, summoned even greater determination, to outsmart and outdo her successful male colleagues. Just keeping up would never have been enough, would never have gotten her noticed, let alone promoted.

But now she'd made it. She'd reached her goal. And what, she wondered soberly, had changed? She was still going to have to prove herself better, smarter, tougher than her new partners. They'd be watching and criticizing her every step. There'd be no resting on her laurels, no smugly sitting back and smelling the roses. As a partner, she was bound to have to work even harder from now on, be even more on her toes.

And Simon would insist on giving her his time and loving support, on making life easier for her—if he didn't come to resent her dedication to her job in time. But he wouldn't…their marriage, his commitment to her, were too important to him, he'd convinced her of that. As long as he felt she needed his emotional and physical backup, he would be there for her.

She gazed pensively into her muesli bowl as she scraped up her last mouthful. Regardless of what he might want himself, she knew he would put *her* needs and well-being first. Even if he had a change of heart and felt the pull back to neurosurgery, she felt sure he'd clamp down on the urge. He wouldn't want to jeopardize their marriage by going back to the demanding, often risky work he'd once loved. And maybe, deep down, still did.

"Ready for some toast now?" Simon asked, his hand hovering over the loaf of sliced bread. There was a faint query in his eyes, and she knew it had nothing to do with bread or toast. He thought she was thinking of her work again, of the weekend ahead with her new partners.

"Um…one slice will do…thanks," she said, her eyes softening as she looked into his. Wanting him to see the love she felt for him. "And *next* weekend," she added firmly, "we're going to have our first golf lesson. We'll buy some clubs during the week. Or on Saturday morning."

"You're on," he said, dropping a slice of bread into the toaster. "I suppose the partners will have golf days occasionally, so you'll need to know how to play when they ask you join them." His lips were smiling, but his eyes were hidden from her now as he poured her a coffee, making her unsure what he was thinking.

"They won't want a female novice muscling in on

their game and mucking it up," she said, knowing how serious Guy Mallaby, for one, was about his golf.

"You'll show 'em. I've no doubt about that." He looked up as he said it, his blue eyes warm, showing nothing but encouragement.

I don't want to show *them,* she thought, her own eyes melting under the warmth of his. I just want a relaxing game of golf with *you,* my darling. The partners would turn it into a competition, a battle for supremacy or, in her case, a battle of the sexes. But she was reluctant to say it aloud, not wanting to sound peevish or disloyal, talking that way about her soon-to-be partners.

"I'd better eat up," she said, grabbing the toast as it popped up. "Then I must finish unpacking, get dressed and call my mother. We'll have to leave around midday."

"The unpacking's all done. I did it while you were still sleeping like a baby. If you can't find anything, just yell."

"Simon," she said, feeling thoroughly spoilt and indulged by now, "you're far too good to me. What can I do for *you?*"

His eyes danced suddenly. "Just go on being here with me…and making wildly passionate love to me, the way you did last night."

She flushed. "That will be too easy. Think of something more difficult."

"Mmm…you could strip down and do a belly dance for me. "

"Dream on. I'd need more flesh around my middle."

"Let me be the judge of that."

She grinned. "Sorry, no time. And the mood's not right. Give me a rain check?" She took a bite of toast and crunched it, very unromantically, right under his nose.

Chapter Eleven

A distinctive blue haze hung over the heavily timbered ranges and craggy, steep-sided valleys of the aptly named Blue Mountains. With Simon driving carefully on the winding road and Annabel following the directions Guy Mallaby had given over the phone, they had no trouble finding the narrow bush track that led to Guy's weekend retreat.

Scratchy eucalyptus branches brushed the windows of their car as they bumped over the uneven track. The pungent scent of gum leaves pervaded the air. Sunlight and shadows flickered by. For an early winter weekend, the weather was promising—crisp and clear.

When Guy's sprawling rustic weekender showed up ahead, Simon gave a grunt that might have meant anything. Approval, satisfaction at finding it or possibly even a stifled groan.

Annabel glanced at him, running anxious eyes over his unreadable profile. "I hope you won't find this weekend a dead bore," she said. These were *her* work colleagues, not his. High-powered lawyers, not dedicated doctors. Different worlds, different interests, different ideals. What if he hated it? What if the partners talked shop the whole time and made him feel out of it, or asked too many prying questions about his changed circumstances? She didn't want anything upsetting him, threatening their newfound happiness, putting a possible wedge between them.

"We're *both* going to enjoy it. Just relax." Simon looked unworried as he swung the car into an open gravel area close to the house. Other cars were already parked there, so they obviously weren't the first to arrive. He slid their modest Toyota into a vacant spot between a shiny BMW and a sleek Alfa Romeo.

Guy Mallaby and his slender, dark-haired wife Susan, hearing their car, were there to meet them as they pulled up. Simon had met them both before, at a glittering black-tie law dinner. Both in their fifties, the still handsome couple looked quite different today in casual jeans and sweaters, with no sign of the suave formality, elaborate grooming or expensive jewelry that had set them apart that night.

"Good to see you, Annabel…Simon. Welcome back to Australia." Beaming, Guy ushered his wife forward. "You remember my wife Susan?"

As Annabel smiled and nodded, Simon held out his hand. "Of course…how are you, Susan?" he said, turning on the charm. The same charm, Annabel mused, that had once made her mistake him for a dashing Italian

Romeo. The devastating smile, the compelling blue gaze, the warmly rumbled greeting that curled through every fibre of a woman's being.

She saw Susan Mallaby actually blush.

"We're happy to have you back in the fold, Annabel," Guy said. "You must be very proud of your wife, Simon…achieving a partnership at such a young age. And flying the flag for women, what's more."

"Extremely proud…and happy for her," Simon agreed, his eyes softening as he looked down at his wife.

He really *is* happy for me, and proud of me, Annabel thought with an uneasy skip of her heart. The more she thought about it, the more convinced she was that he was giving up his own career—his beloved neurosurgery—for *her*…for the sake of their marriage…so that their two demanding careers wouldn't conflict, and consume them as they had before.

She opened her mouth to point out that she wasn't a partner yet, but shut it again, thinking of what she'd achieved. Damn it, a partnership was what she'd longed for, worked so hard for. She ought to be happy, too, enjoying her moment of glory. She *was* happy. She'd proved to herself, to the world and, above all, to her doubting parents—she'd weakened and told her mother about her offer this morning, knowing she'd pass the news on to her father—that she could mix it with the high-flying males at the top.

Now she was there, she mustn't rest on her laurels or even think of turning down the offer and throwing it all away. Her hard-won triumph, the sacrifices she'd made, would have been in vain. And even more unbearable to contemplate, it would mean that the time and loving care she'd denied her baby daughter in her furious drive to reach her goal and prove something to herself and her parents would have been a sinful, worthless waste.

"Let me take your overnight bags." Guy reached into the backseat and dragged out their two bags, stuffed with walking boots and sturdy bush gear. "We're putting you in the guest bungalow with the Dwyers. The others are staying at a motel down the road."

"We could stay at—" Annabel began to protest, not wanting priority treatment. She wasn't a partner *yet*.

But that was as far as she got. "Nonsense, you're special guests. It's our way of welcoming you back." With Susan leading the way, Guy waved them into the house. "I'll show you your room before we join the others on the terrace. Everyone's here now except the Dwyers, our birthday boy Matt and his wife and young son."

Minutes later, emerging from the house, Annabel found herself swamped by smiling faces and outstretched arms. It was a heart-warming welcome, made easier by the fact that she knew most of the gathered throng already, having worked with these same lawyers up until two years ago, and having already met a few of their wives, as well. She kept Simon's arm tightly wedged in her own so he wouldn't be ignored or overlooked.

Ignored? Overlooked? No fear of *that!* One of the younger women—one she *hadn't* met before—gave a delighted squeal and launched herself at Simon before the man at her side could introduce her.

"Simon Pacino!" she cried, drawing curious eyes

their way. "Oh, what a wonderful, amazing surprise! I thought you were still overseas."

Annabel tried to keep a smile plastered to her face, but it was difficult. The woman was a knockout, a stunningly attractive, voluptuous redhead with startling amber eyes—and right at this moment, she had eyes for no one but Simon, as if they'd shared...what? And *when?*

She let her uncertain gaze flicker to the tall, bespectacled man hovering behind. Damien Harris—the youngest partner in the firm, still a bachelor when she'd last seen him nearly two years ago. He looked as startled, as bewildered, as she felt herself. And when she flicked a glance back at the redhead, she could understand why. The amber-eyed siren wore a glittering, obviously new engagement ring on her long red-tipped ring finger. No wonder Damien was looking dazed. His brand-new fiancée falling all over another man!

And Simon, she saw, was nodding amiably, lapping it up. He knew this alluring sexpot all right. Knew her *well,* by the look of it. And not a twinge of discomfort was he showing!

"Lorelei...good to see you again."

Lorelei... Annabel rolled her eyes. *Siren of the Rhine...*how appropriate! For once, the sight of Simon turning on the charm left her cold. She felt like withdrawing her arm from his, but found she couldn't. Now he was the one clamping *her* arm in a wedge-like grip, despite the fact that Lorelei was clawing at his *other* arm.

"And you, Simon," the young woman gushed. "Meeting like this is unbelievable! Damien, honey..."

She whirled round, her lovely face aglow. "You must meet Simon Pacino, the most amazing, caring, *wonderful* man who ever walked this earth."

Amazing…caring…wonderful…Annabel's head spun. She was conscious of eyes widening, partners grinning and nudging each other, one or two of the men seizing the excuse to openly ogle the flame-haired siren.

"Simon is the brilliant neurosurgeon who saved my mother's life!"

As Lorelei paused for dramatic effect, an impressed hum rose from the crowd, Damien's face cleared, and Annabel felt the tension sliding from her body.

Lorelei, fully aware that she was the center of attention, raised her lilting voice so that everyone could hear. "My mother had a brain tumor three years ago. The so-called experts told us it was inoperable. But Simon felt she had a chance. And now she's completely better. It was a miracle! And we have Simon to thank."

Simon was shaking his head now, even frowning a little. Now Annabel could feel *his* tension. He'd be hating this focus on him, this fuss over a past triumph. In his eyes, a single personal tragedy had obliterated all his previous successes.

But Lorelei wasn't taking the hint. Maybe she hadn't heard about Lily, about what had happened two years ago. Or maybe she felt her mother's miraculous recovery overrode that single unfortunate failure and was worth shouting about.

"We heard you'd gone overseas, after an injury to your hand…" Lorelei cast a sympathetic look downward and seemed satisfied his injury was fully healed. "But now you're back! Are you back at your old hospital?"

"No," Simon said curtly, using the tone he'd used in the past to discourage further questions. "I'll be working in research. I'm glad your mother is well, Lorelei. Please give her my regards." His lips eased into a smile. Only Annabel could sense the pain underneath. He'd lost his own mother to a brain tumor, knowing that with better care she could have been saved. And years later, he'd failed to save his mortally injured baby daughter, refusing to accept that she was already beyond help.

"Excuse us, Lorelei. Damien." Simon began to back away, expecting Lorelei to release him and drop her hand. "I'd better get my wife a drink."

The claw-like grip on his arm tightened. "You're going into *research?*" Lorelei was hearing only what she wanted to hear, refusing to be sidetracked. Damien, looking uncomfortable, tugged at her arm, but she wasn't budging.

"But you can't have given up neurosurgery, Simon!" Lorelei's beautiful face screwed up in outrage. "You've saved so many lives, given hope to so many people. You're the best neurosurgeon in Australia. Everyone says so!" She caught her breath, seeming finally to sense the tension rising from Simon. "Oh dear! You didn't give up surgery because you lost your baby daughter, did you?"

As a shocked hush fell over the assembled guests, Lorelei's amber eyes widened in sympathy. "It must have been terrible for you, Simon. I heard you were forced to operate, but your daughter was beyond even your help. That hit-and-run car thief should be strung up!"

"Lorelei, darling…" Damien looked as if he wanted

to sink into the earth at his feet—and take her with him. "This isn't the—"

"Here we are, everyone! Our birthday boy's arrived." Guy Mallaby's voice boomed from the doorway of the house. Annabel seized the chance to escape, plucking Simon from Lorelei's grasp and dragging him across the terrace to the outdoor bar.

Her eyes met his for an anxious second as he poured her a glass of punch and snatched up a beer for himself. He looked more relieved at escaping Lorelei than upset, she was glad to see, as if he'd prepared himself for insensitive remarks from people who'd heard about his past, and was refusing to let it bother him. Yet for a second, it *had.* She wondered if Lorelei's effusive praise on behalf of her mother and her palpable dismay over Simon giving up neurosurgery had touched a nerve with him, perhaps even making him think twice about what he was giving up.

Or maybe that was just wishful thinking.

"Come on, Matt…Molly…and you, too, young Robbie." Guy Mallaby was steering his latest guests and their snowy-haired son onto the paved terrace, to mingle with the other guests, Matt receiving backslaps and birthday wishes as they moved around. Before long, they were heading for Simon and Annabel, who'd moved away to inspect the fish in a rock pond.

"Simon, let me introduce you to Matt Dwyer and his delightful family." Guy waved them forward. "Annabel, you know Matt and Molly already, of course."

As Annabel greeted the couple warmly, wishing Matt a happy birthday, Simon stepped forward to shake hands. While they were exchanging pleasantries, Guy put an arm round their little boy and thrust him forward. "You may not have met Matt and Molly's young son, Robbie. He's just turned six, he tells me."

Annabel looked down at the rosy-cheeked boy with his mop of snow-white hair, smiled, and said warmly, "Hi, Robbie. My, you're a big boy now. Six years old!" As she straightened, she sensed a stiffening in the man beside her. Glancing up at him, she saw the blood had drained from Simon's face. With everyone looking down at Robbie with indulgent smiles, only she would be aware of the change in him.

He might have seen a ghost! Was Robbie an ex-patient? Had Simon operated on the boy at some time in the past, and not expected him to survive long-term? Or did Robbie remind him of a child he'd lost under the knife—perhaps even Lily, who'd had fair hair, too—stirring up painful, unwanted memories?

Or was it just being in the company of a child? Since losing his daughter, he'd avoided children, avoided any contact with them, even to the extent of declining to operate on young children, referring them when he could to other neurosurgeons.

She saw his chest rise and fall as he heaved in a breath and released it, as if making an effort to cover up his reaction before anyone noticed anything amiss.

"Good to meet you, Robbie." He thrust out a hand and swallowed the boy's small hand in his. "Robbie is short for Robert, is it?"

His voice, Annabel thought, had an unnatural ring to it, but again, only she—someone who knew him well—would have noticed.

Did even *she* know him well? Simon had secrets,

hidden demons; she'd sensed that more than once. Secrets he kept even from her. Secrets that could possibly threaten their marriage in the future if he couldn't bring himself to share them with her.

"No, it's not." The boy looked up at Simon with a sassy grin, as if to say, *You think you're smart, mister, but you're not!* "It's short for Robin!"

"Ah. Robin, eh? That's a good name." And Simon actually smiled back—as tender a smile as she'd ever seen. It came as a surprise. A *pleasant* surprise. Simon still liked children, could still warm to them, communicate with them. She'd begun to despair that he'd ever feel comfortable with a child again.

They all laughed, and Guy and the young family of three drifted off, to catch up with other friends. Annabel hesitated a moment before sliding a look up at Simon. She asked tentatively, "You looked for a moment as if you'd met Robbie before."

"Did I?" He looked startled. "Um…no…never. I guess he just reminded me for a second of…some kid I knew once."

"A patient?"

"No…not a patient." His face closed up as she watched, his blue eyes turning remote, as if he were deliberately wiping out any emotion, any pain, any feeling that might have been there. He was shutting her out again. He didn't want her to ask, to probe. Especially not here, not now.

But would he tell her later? She sighed and looked away. Not without her teasing or dragging it out of him, she suspected. And not here in a stranger's house, with reminders of his past right here under the same roof. She might as well just forget it and try to enjoy the week-end…and hope that he could enjoy it, too.

"Let's go mingle," she suggested brightly, and he seemed happy to go along, even bending to brush her lips with the warmth of his, as if to thank her for not pressing him.

The rest of the afternoon and evening did turn out to be fun. The succulent barbecue steaks, sizzling sausages and homemade rissoles, the salads and other delicacies, the champagne toasts for Matt's fortieth birthday and more toasts for her own return and "bright future with Mallaby's," the upbeat music from a compact disc player and even some dancing on the terrace kept the ball rolling well into the evening. Flickering braziers kept the cold evening air at bay.

Robbie wasn't the only child there. There were two older children, a brother and sister, around ten and twelve years old. Towheaded Robbie, a highly energetic, seemingly tireless little boy, had no trouble keeping up with them. He had an adventurous streak that lured him close to the surrounding bush more than once, keeping his parents and the older children perpetually on their toes.

Annabel noticed Simon watching Robbie, too, from a distance, and wondered if he was being protective of the boy or simply reliving some haunting memory from his past. But she bit her lip and said nothing. Surely, when he learned to trust her again, to trust her fully, he would open up of his own accord. Now that they would be making more time for each other, they'd grow closer, hopefully, as the days went by.

* * *

Simon held his wife close as they swayed in time to the low, sultry tones of a liquid-voiced blues singer. Annabel had her eyes closed and was humming softly, contentedly, as if she was happy being with him. As if she was where she most wanted to be…in his arms. In his life.

He brushed her soft hair with his lips, hoping she would always feel that way. And doubting, darkly, that she would. Once she knew what he was going to have to tell her.

He'd been silently kicking himself all evening. He ought to have controlled himself better, not reacted so pathetically to the sight of a child he'd never met. But that snow-white hair…the cheeky little face…the name *Robbie,* for heaven's sake! It brought it all back…the grinding shame and remorse…the unbearable belief that he was a monster…his father's violent reaction, his brutal rejection…and, above all, the gut-wrenching guilt he'd buried for so long…that his mother had *forced* him to bury.

But he couldn't keep it buried anymore. He couldn't go on hiding the ugly truth about himself, refusing to confront it and admit what he had done. For most of his life—even more so since Lily's death—it had been like a gnawing cancer inside him, eating at him, a constant torture that refused to go away. He had to tell Annabel, even if she despised him for it, and viciously rejected him, too

She'd sensed there was something wrong this afternoon, but she'd backed off without pressing him. It would be so easy to leave it at that…buried…forgotten…the way his mother had insisted it had to be. But what kind of man would he be, what kind of husband, if he couldn't own up to the biggest mistake—worse, the most sinful act—of his life?

He gritted his teeth. Forget about betraying his mother's trust, disobeying a deathbed promise... He couldn't hide behind a childhood vow forever, refusing to face up to what he had done. Damn it, he couldn't live with it any more.

He had to tell her...even though it would mean exposing himself in his worst possible light. Even if it meant peeling away his darkest, ugliest layers and revealing his painfully true colors to the woman he loved more than anything in the world—a woman he'd already driven away once.

He felt the warmth of her slender body moving against his, felt her heart flutter under his own, and his will faltered. How could he bear to risk losing her again? Why should he take such a gamble, expose the ugly truth, when nobody other than himself knew or need ever know?

He knew...that was why. And damn it, his father, if he was still alive, *he* knew, too Not that he cared what his father thought of him. He only cared about Annabel...how *she* would react. His lip curled in self-contempt. Simon Pacino, who'd gained the respect of his peers and the gratitude, even love, of many of his ex-patients, was living a lie, pretending to be someone he wasn't, holding a vital part of himself from his wife...a betrayal in itself.

It couldn't go on. It would always be there between them, a constant torment, and she would sense it. She *had* sensed...something.

The moment they were alone again, back in Sydney, he would sit her down and tell her. And hope she could still love him enough to forgive him.

But could he expect even a loving wife to forgive what his own father had called malicious, cold-blooded murder?

Chapter Twelve

After a hearty country breakfast the next morning, Guy addressed the small group gathered on the terrace. "Okay, listen up, folks. Is this everyone who's coming on the bush walk?"

A few of the wives, including Susan Mallaby, were staying behind in the warmth for a lazy chat, and the couple with the two older children had already left for Sydney, having their son's football game to attend.

"Lorelei will be here in a minute." Damien Harris looked resigned, as if used to his fiancée running late.

"Right." Guy hitched a knapsack over his shoulder. A first aid kit, presumably, if the red cross on it was any indication. "Matt, are you sure young Robbie will be able to keep up?"

Matt Dwyer shot a wry grin at his jiggling son. "Are

you kidding? Robbie's inexhaustible. Never stops. We'll have trouble keeping up with *him*."

"Okay." Guy wandered around, looking them over. "Do you all have tough, comfortable walking shoes? Or boots? And warm jackets in case the weather deteriorates before we get back?"

So far the weather was holding up well—the sky still clear, the sun already bright, though with little warmth as yet after an early morning frost.

"All ready to go," said Annabel, suppressing a yawn, wishing she'd gone to bed earlier and had more sleep.

Her body was still tingling from Simon's tempestuous lovemaking last night in the Mallabys' bungalow. He'd swept her up in a storm of incredible sensation, as if there were no tomorrow. Conscious of the thin walls and the Dwyer family in the room next door, she'd managed to muffle her cries in the hollow of his throat, but it hadn't been easy. She'd wanted to moan and scream at the top of her lungs.

The passion and fury of his lovemaking had left her shaken. There was a desperate edge to it, as if he wasn't expecting their newfound happiness to last. Surely he wasn't afraid that she'd run out on him again?

"Here I am," cooed a lilting voice. "Haven't kept you waiting, have I?"

All eyes swung round as Lorelei sashayed onto the terrace, looking dewy fresh and as eye-catching as ever in a bright red parka and a red, blue and gold woollen cap pulled low over her flaming hair.

Annabel had half expected her to stay behind for a lazy gossip with the wives in the warmth of the house.

Maybe she just preferred being around males. They certainly loved being around *her.*

But Lorelei, she noticed, was only paying attention to one man, and it wasn't her dark-haired, bespectacled fiancé.

"Simon," Lorelei gurgled, advancing on Annabel's husband with a purposeful gleam in her eye and a camera in her hand. "Mind if I take a couple of photographs of you for my mother? She'd love to have them. She'll be thrilled to hear I've met up with you."

Simon backed up a step. "I'm not a good…I'd prefer…" He tossed an appealing glance at his wife, plainly hoping she would back him up, get him out of it. He'd always resisted having his photograph taken, being singled out, pinned down, made a fuss of.

But Annabel just waved a hand and said, "Oh, Simon, it's just a photo for a grateful patient. Lorelei's mother owes you her life. Just smile."

Simon grimaced. "You come and be in it, too. You're my wife."

As she hesitated, Lorelei was quick to make the decision. "I'll take one of you and your wife afterwards," she said, and pointed her camera at Simon. "Say cheese!"

"Cheese," Simon said dryly, giving a reluctant smile, not for Lorelei but for her mother. The camera clicked.

"One more, just to make sure." Another click. "Thank you, Simon, that's great. Ooh, they're leaving us behind," Lorelei squeaked as she saw Guy and the others heading off. "Come on, Damien!" Grabbing her fiancé's arm, she scuttled after them.

Simon and Annabel exchanged rueful glances as

they followed in their wake. Lorelei had what she wanted, a photo of Simon. Simon's wife was forgotten.

They soon found themselves deep in the bush, with a steep rocky slope on one side and a thick forest of eucalyptus and other native trees on the other. Bird sounds rang from the branches. Twigs snapped underfoot. The air was cold, fresh and invigorating.

"Make sure you stick to the path," Guy shouted as his group spread out along the bush track. "We don't want anyone getting lost."

"Robbie, you stay in sight!" Matt Dwyer yelled out as his snowy-headed son galloped on ahead. "You see why Molly needed a rest," he added with a grin. His wife had chosen to stay behind. With a live-wire son like Robbie, Annabel guessed she'd need all the rest she could get.

Simon touched Matt's arm. "I'll keep him in sight. You stay and talk to Annabel." He strode on ahead.

"Thanks," Matt called after him. He fell into step beside Annabel. "Thoughtful husband you have there. He's good with children, isn't he?"

Annabel nodded, swallowing a lump in her throat. She could almost tell what Matt was thinking, or what he wanted to ask next. *Think you'll have any more?* She braced herself to answer, *I hope so,* and realized that really was what she longed for. Another child. *Simon's* child.

She sighed, and was relieved when Matt didn't ask the question. Because how could she answer for Simon? It wasn't something they'd talked about, been *able* to talk about. Not yet.

Sadly, she couldn't see him ever wanting another child. Wanting to take the risk of being grievously hurt again.

Her eyes narrowed as she strained to see ahead. Both Simon and the boy had disappeared from sight behind a bend in the path. But after seeing the way he'd watched over young Robbie last night, she knew that Simon would never let anything happen to the boy. The tiny dynamo was in good hands with her husband.

She blinked. An apparition—a tall, two-headed monster—loomed into view up ahead. Her vision cleared as it drew closer, taking on a shape that made sense.

It was Simon, with young Robbie sitting proudly aloft on his broad shoulders!

"Well, look at that!" Matt gave a cheer. "My son, it seems, has a new hero. One who knows how to control him."

Lorelei brushed past both of them with her camera at the ready. "I must get a shot of this." She snapped them and turned to grin at the others. "Is it any wonder my mother adores Simon? He's so good with people. I can't imagine why he's thinking of going into—*ouch!*" With a howl, she gripped her ankle, dropping her camera into the grass. "Darn it, I've twisted my ankle!"

"I'm coming, honey!" Damien ran to his injured fiancée. "Sit down on the track. Let me have a—"

"Oh, Damien, darling, you're not a doctor." She waved him away. "Get Simon. He'll know if it's broken or not. *Simon!*" she called out. Even with her voice raised, she managed an appealing tinkling note. "I need your help!"

Annabel knew she'd get it, too. Gallant Simon was always ready to help damsels in distress. She'd seen him in action…on the Grand Canal in Venice, when he'd leapt into the water to rescue *her.*

She watched as he lowered Robbie carefully from his shoulders. Rather than just tossing the boy carelessly aside to play the big hero and attend to Lorelei, as some men might have done, he set the boy down safely on the track first, patting Robbie on the shoulder before moving away.

"I hope I haven't broken it," Lorelei moaned as Simon ran expert hands over her ankle and tested her foot, before carefully removing her boot and woollen sock. Annabel noticed a couple of the partners ogling the girl's shapely ankle, as if they'd never seen a bare ankle before.

"I've a bandage in my first aid kit if you need it," said Guy from behind.

"Thanks," said Simon. "Mmm…it's not swollen. That's a good sign." He felt around a bit more, and then straightened. "I'd say you've just sprained it, Lorelei. Probably best not to walk on it for a while. Your fiancé can help you back to the house. All right, Damien?"

"I'll carry her back," Damien said at once.

Lorelei gave her tinkling laugh. "*You,* carry *me?* I'd like to see that! Look, I'll be all right in a minute. Just put a bandage on my ankle, Simon, and I'll try to put my boot back on." She gazed up at him with her languorous cat's eyes. "Then I'll test it."

Guy handed a bandage to a stoic-faced Simon, who took Lorelei's foot in his hands—his gentle, healing surgeon's hands, Annabel mused, remembering those same hands on her body last night—before setting to work to bind up the girl's ankle. Expertly, like everything he did.

"It's feeling better already." Lorelei gave a contented sigh. "You have wonderful hands, Simon. No wonder you're such a great surgeon."

Annabel expected a curt, *Not anymore,* but he let it go. Maybe to avoid further debate on the subject. He simply concentrated on the task at hand, his face stonily impassive, afterwards peeling Lorelei's sock over the bandage and easing on her boot.

Then he glanced up and frowned. "Is anyone keeping an eye on Robbie?"

Matt jerked round as if stung, dropping Lorelei's camera, which he'd picked up for her. He scanned the track with anxious eyes. No little boy in sight. "Oh, heck, where is the little blighter? Molly will kill me if he gets lost in the bush. *Robbie!*" he yelled at the top of his voice. *"Robbie, come back here!"*

Just as he was about to rush off, a shrill laugh echoed from somewhere above. "Ha ha! I'm the king of the castle! Look, Daddy, look at me!"

Matt glanced up. "Oh, my God," he whispered. His wiry son had climbed up the steep rugged slope onto a narrow rock ledge high above the track. The ledge jutted out like a poking tongue, with no visible support underneath. And Robbie was standing on the edge!

"Don't move, Robbie. I'm coming up!"

"No!" Guy said sharply, stopping Matt dead. "It's not stable up there. There are loose rocks. It won't take your weight. Just order him down! Make him back up carefully and climb down the hill again. He's light...he can do it on his own. Just get him off that ledge first... carefully! Without scaring him."

Matt sucked in a tense breath. "Robbie..." A hoarse croak came out. "Move back off that rock...very, very slowly."

Robbie giggled. He knew everyone was watching

him. It was his big moment. "Look at me, look at me!" he chanted. "I'm the king of the castle!" He started to jig up and down.

"Robbie, be careful!" Matt screamed out, looking ready to leap up the hill regardless.

"Let me…" Simon put a hand on his shoulder. "We're good buddies. Robbie might listen to his new mate."

Annabel swallowed. *Good buddies…new mate.* This was the closest Simon had come to a child, had connected with a child, since…Lily. But had Robbie connected with *him?* Enough to do as Simon told him?

Simon, his face as strained as Matt's, his jaw clenched, looked up at the little boy jiggling about on the precarious rock ledge. "Robbie, it's time to come down now, mate…very carefully." His voice carried easily in the still morning air. "I want you to do just as I say…just as your Daddy has told you…"

Robbie gave a broad grin and stopped his jiggling, ready to listen to his new mate, his good buddy.

But it was already too late. This was made frighteningly clear by an ominous rumbling sound, in the sudden movement and collapsing of rock, stones and earth. The rock ledge holding Robbie seemed to fold in on itself, splitting in two before tumbling down the hill in a roar of loosened rocks, earth, pebbles and dust, swallowing the boy in an unstoppable, terrifying landslide.

Matt gave a strangled shriek. Lorelei leapt back with a bloodcurdling scream, her sore ankle forgotten. Her shocked fiancé shouted, "Move back! Move back!" The others stood watching in horror, more concerned for Matt's helpless son than their own safety.

Matt and Simon leapt into action the moment the tumbling earth and rocks stopped their downward slide, the air falling silent, heavy with flying dust. Robbie was nowhere in sight, buried somewhere beneath the rocks, earth and rubble. Moaning his son's name, Matt started hauling rocks aside.

"Careful," Simon cautioned, using his own powerful arms and shoulders to shift rocks. "Make sure they're safe to move first. Robbie could be trapped underneath any of them."

As the others scrambled to help, digging with their hands among the earth and rubble, Guy pulled out his mobile phone. "I'll call for a rescue helicopter. An ambulance would never be able to get in here." Nobody told him it might already be too late.

"He's here, he's here!" The hoarse cry came from Matt. "Oh, God, he's wedged under this rock! Robbie, you'll be all right, tiger. Daddy's here." He looked up at Simon with fear in his eyes. "He's not moving! You're a doctor. Is he…is he…? Is it safe to shift this rock off him?"

Simon dropped to his knees beside the trapped boy. "He's unconscious, not dead. He still has a pulse. Yes, help me get it off him quickly. He's having trouble breathing."

"This is all my fault," Lorelei moaned as the two men eased the rock from the small limp figure. "If I hadn't hurt my stupid ankle, Robbie would never have had the chance to climb up that hill!"

"It's not your fault, honey," Damien consoled, wiping a streak of dirt from her cheek. "The kid can move like greased lightning!"

"He's not moving now," Lorelei groaned.

"Hush…please." Annabel spoke softly but sharply, without looking round. Her eyes were fixed to Simon as he bent over the child. She didn't want anything distracting him, anything going wrong. *Anything he could blame himself for.*

"He can't breathe." Simon's head came up sharply. "I'll need to do a tracheotomy." She noted how pale and tense his face was, noted the steely glitter in his eyes. "I need to clear his airway. Fast. He'll die if I don't." She heard the tightness in his voice and felt a stab of fear, for him, for herself, for their marriage. If he failed… "Anyone got a knife?" he rapped out. "And an air tube of some kind? A pen'll do…hurry!" He was peeling aside Robbie's jacket and shirt as he spoke.

"I've got a knife." Guy burrowed into his first aid kit. "Here." He thrust it at Simon.

"And I've a pen when you're ready," Damien said. "I'll empty it and make it into a tube."

"Right. Matt!" Simon rasped without looking up. "Press a pad of some kind over the wound on Robbie's head. You must stop the bleeding while I'm…" His voice trailed off. He was already cutting into the tender flesh above Robbie's sternum. Annabel gulped, but didn't draw her gaze away. Or stop silently praying— for Simon as much as for Robbie.

"Lorelei, not now!" hissed Guy from behind.

Now Annabel did glance round. And had to choke back an affronted cry. Lorelei was taking photographs of Simon as he worked on Robbie to save his life! If she hadn't been afraid of wrecking her husband's concentration, Annabel would have leapt up and torn the camera from the girl's grasp.

Poor Simon, she thought, hoping he was concentrating too hard to hear what was going on behind him. He would *hate* it, being photographed at a crucial time like this. And if anything went wrong...*dear heaven, what would it do to him?*

"He's breathing!" Matt cried. A jubilant cry. "Simon, you've saved my son's life!"

"There's still his head injury," Simon said grimly, but Annabel caught a flicker of emotion in his eyes and sensed his relief. Robbie *would* have died if Simon hadn't acted so quickly and competently, and Simon knew it. He had done what he knew had to be done.

"Keep that pad on his wound, Matt, while I examine him." Simon was peeling off his own jacket now, laying it over the boy for extra warmth.

Nobody spoke or moved as he checked the boy's vital signs, examined his pupils and inspected his tiny skull with gentle fingers, feeling beneath his dusty mop of hair for fractures or swelling, lifting the bloodied pad to inspect the scalp wound. Finally, he ran his hands over the child's limbs and body. Robbie lay like a limp doll, still ominously unconscious.

"Is he...going to be all right?" Matt hardly dared to ask.

"His body will heal," Simon was able to say with confidence. "But his head injury..." A spasm crossed his taut features. "Is that helicopter on its way? We need to get him to a hospital...fast. He has a possible fractured skull and some swelling. He needs a CT scan, and maybe an operation."

"Will you do it?" Matt asked at once.

Annabel held her breath. "I don't do surgery anymore," Simon said, his voice tight. But there was something in his eyes...a yearning? A regret? *Did he secretly long to operate on this little boy who had touched him for some reason? Was he beginning to miss using the skills he'd trained so hard to perfect?*

"But I'd like to fly with him to the hospital, if it's okay with you and the paramedics." Simon said, bending over the boy again. "He'll need close watching."

Expert watching, he meant, Annabel thought, wondering what all this was doing to Simon. Having another child's life in his hands. A child he'd singled out, for some reason, from the moment he'd set eyes on him.

"I'll insist you go with them," Matt readily agreed. "And you must be present if they have to operate. As an observer. I'll insist on that, too"

Simon made no comment to that.

"A helicopter's on its way," Guy Mallaby reported, his mobile phone to his ear. He'd been quietly talking into it for some time. "It won't be long. They're going to take him straight to Sydney. To the Children's Hospital."

The Children's Hospital... Annabel swallowed. The hospital where Simon had wanted to send Lily, only there hadn't been time, leaving him no choice but to operate himself, despite knowing in his heart that it was already too late. She flicked him an anxious look.

A jaw muscle twitched, his only discernible reaction. His eyes were hidden from her. When he spoke, his voice was calm. "Good. We mustn't move him till a stretcher is winched down."

"Thank God you both came back to Australia when you did," Guy said with feeling. "We would have lost him if you hadn't been here, Simon."

As Simon glanced up, the morning sun slanted into his face. His eyes glittered with an emotion that shook Annabel, as if he realized he'd finally saved the life of a child, a child he'd come to feel a special bond with, and he couldn't quite accept it. But all he said was, "With phone instructions, you could have done it."

Guy looked horrified. He didn't believe it. None of them believed it.

Annabel drove back to Sydney alone, her mind in turmoil. Matt and Molly had sped on ahead, desperate to get to the hospital. Matt had trusted Simon to travel with his son in the helicopter. He'd trusted Simon to be the one his son saw first if he woke during the flight.

People trusted Simon, relied on him to take care of them and their loved ones. Did Simon realize it? He inspired confidence, admiration and respect in people. Even love, she thought, thinking of Robbie and Lorelei's mother and other patients he'd saved. He'd be wasted in a sterile research laboratory, with no contact with people or patients, where there'd be no need for his expert practical and surgical skills.

After seeing the yearning look in her husband's eyes when Matt Dwyer had begged him to operate on his son, she was convinced that Simon's old passion was flickering anew, that he was missing surgery and secretly longing to go back to it. It was no longer the memory of Lily that was preventing him going back, it was *her*. His wife. Her career. Her promotion to a partnership.

He was determined to be there for her, to lighten her workload and avoid the stresses of juggling two conflicting careers. Even if it meant sacrificing his own brilliant career. He would give up his dream, his love of surgery, for *her,* to ensure their lives were happy and their marriage kept intact.

She gripped the steering wheel, emotion quivering through her. Was her own career worth his sacrifice?

Simon had told her to go straight home and wait for him there, but she headed for the hospital instead. No matter how long it took, she wanted to be there for him if the news about Robbie was bad…or if they had to operate and weren't able to save him. That could plunge Simon back into the abyss, convincing him he'd done the right thing in giving up surgery for good. But she knew that in his heart…in his deepest heart…

Oh dear God, Robbie had to be all right.

She found Matt and Molly in the corridor outside the operating room, holding on to one another as if trying to absorb each other's strength. But they looked up and smiled when they saw her, doing their best to put on brave faces.

"No news yet?" she asked tentatively, sitting down beside Molly, hoping they wouldn't resent her intrusion.

"He's still unconscious." It was Matt who answered, his voice heavy. "He's had X-rays and scans. They have to operate to remove a clot."

She felt Molly shudder, and put a comforting hand on her arm. "He's an amazingly strong little boy," she said, not knowing what else to say.

"Yes…it's a miracle he survived the fall," Molly said huskily. She turned to her. "Are you looking for Simon?"

She hesitated. "I…just wanted to be here. Have you seen him?"

"He's in the operating room," Matt told her.

"You mean   " Her heart flared for a second.

"He's not doing the surgery," Matt said with a regret-ful twist of his lip. "But they've invited him to be there. I had a word with the chief neurosurgeon. He's a friend of Simon's." His eyes glistened with emotion. "Every-one knows Simon saved Robbie's life. And that he kept Robbie alive in the helicopter. We owe your husband a lot."

Annabel gulped. Matt's eyes told her that they'd still be grateful to Simon, even if their son didn't come through the operation or survive the effects of his head trauma. She hoped Simon would realize it, hoped that Matt would make sure he did.

"Can I get you some coffee?" she offered. "And a sandwich?"

"Just coffee, thanks." Neither wanted to eat, and An-nabel couldn't blame them. She knew she wouldn't be able to swallow food right now either.

Guy and Susan arrived half an hour later, with Lore-lei and Damien in their wake. Lorelei had her camera slung over her shoulder, but made no attempt to use it. Time dragged on. Lorelei and Damien eventually drifted off, and after a while Guy and Susan left, too, promising to keep in touch.

After what seemed endless hours, a tall figure in a green theatre gown emerged from the operating room. Annabel's eyes flew to the man's face, hoping it would be Simon, yet dreading what he might have to tell them.

But it wasn't Simon, it was Marcus Greenway, the neurosurgeon. She'd met him once at a medical dinner. He looked serious, but smiled when he saw their anxious faces. "He's come through the operation," he said, "and he's awake. He actually smiled when he saw Simon. That's a good sign."

"You're saying…he's going to be all right?" Molly asked hoarsely.

"It's a bit early to say what the long-term effects might be. He'll need close watching for a while, but the early signs are good. He's a tough kid. His padded jacket probably saved him from injuries to his body and limbs, apart from a few grazes and bruises. Simon's treatment at the scene undoubtedly saved his life. You're Simon's wife, aren't you?" he asked, noticing Annabel.

She nodded. "Annabel," she reminded him. "Is Simon still in there with Robbie?"

"Yes. He wants to stay with him overnight. The first twenty-four hours are critical, and I've said he can. They'll wheel Robbie out in a minute to go to the recovery room." He turned to Molly and Matt. "After you've seen him you can either go home and have a good night's sleep, or we'll provide beds here."

"Thank you, doctor. We'll stay here." Molly was suddenly looking ten years younger. "I have so much to thank you for. You and Simon."

"I think Simon deserves the thanks. If he hadn't saved your son's life in the first place…" The surgeon pursed his lips, glancing at Annabel. "He belongs back in neurosurgery. I told him so. But he seems intent on switching to research."

Annabel drew in her breath and said nothing. If today's events hadn't changed his mind, what would? She let her breath out in a sigh.

"Here they come now," Marcus Greenway said, and left them to it.

Molly and Matt rushed to the trolley as a nurse wheeled it out. Simon, his tanned skin stretched tight over his cheekbones, still showing the strain he'd been under, trailed behind.

Molly gripped Matt's arm. Their son looked so tiny lying there, his head swathed in white bandages, with no sign of his mop of snowy hair, his eyes closed, his small face poignantly pale.

"Is he unconscious again?" Molly asked, looking anxiously at Simon.

Simon dragged his eyes from Annabel's. "No, he's sleeping normally. The nurses will wake him now and then to check his vital signs. Mind if I stay with him overnight, Molly? Just to be sure."

"Oh thank you, Simon, we'd be so grateful if you would."

Annabel flicked her tongue over her lips. *Just to be sure,* he'd said. To be sure there was an expert close by, watching over him, just in case, she thought. He knew how precarious the little boy's condition still was and how overworked the nurses were. Simon was still treating Robbie as if he were personally responsible for him, as if the boy was still his patient. Robbie, for some reason, had touched him in a special way. *A child other than Lily had become special to him.* She wished she knew why.

"You won't mind if I stay here overnight, Bel?" Simon asked her. His eyes seemed to be saying more, but she wasn't sure just what. There was a glint of urgency in the blue depths, an edginess in him, that made her heart skip a beat. Did he have something he wanted to tell her—*had he decided he wanted to go back to surgery after all?*—or was it just that he couldn't wait to have her to himself again, to hold her in his arms and blot out today's trauma?

"You stay as long as you need to," she said, her voice husky. "I'll be waiting at home for you. Guy told me to take tomorrow off, not to come in until Tuesday. Is there anything you need before I go?"

"Anything I need I can get myself." He smiled, a special smile just for her that curled round her heart and melted her bones. "You go home and get some sleep," he said. "I'll be home in the morning."

Again there was that look in his eye, that gleam of…what? Purpose? Determination? She didn't know whether to be excited or worried.

She was having breakfast the next morning when she heard a car door slam. She opened the front door and saw a taxi speed off. Simon was striding toward her. His face and body language told her something was wrong. Robbie? She looked closer. It wasn't grief or sadness she saw, it was anger. *Blazing* anger.

Her heart sank. Was he angry at himself? Angry that after all his efforts, after using all the skills at his disposal yesterday, he'd lost Robbie—and let them all down? Was he blaming himself again?

She held out a hand to him, but he thrust past her and slammed something down on the kitchen bench.

"Look what she's done!" he exploded. "The bitch has sold her damned photographs to the tabloids!"

"Simon, what—?" She looked down at the newspaper. It was a copy of the *Sydney Morning Herald*—with Simon's photograph on the front page! HERO DOCTOR SAVES BOY'S LIFE was emblazoned across the top in bold letters. Underneath, in smaller print, it read: *Renowned neurosurgeon Simon Pacino performs a life-saving tracheotomy on a six-year-old boy caught in a landslide in the Blue Mountains.* MORE ON PAGE 5.

Her eyes widened. It showed Simon smiling into the camera, posing rather stiffly for the photograph that graced the front page of Sydney's popular daily newspaper. It was the photograph Lorelei had said she wanted for her mother!

"Is it any damned wonder I—"

"Simon, calm down," she begged. "You *are* a hero. She shouldn't have used your photograph without your permission, but—"

"Hero? *Hero!*" he fumed, savagely rejecting the notion. "I haven't tried to save lives to make a *hero* of myself, for pity's sake! Whatever good I've done in my life, I've done to make up for...*hell, I could never make up for what I did. Never!*"

Her heart slowed almost to a stop. "Simon, what are you saying? Tell me!" Whatever it was, he had to deal with it, then let it go. It was tearing him apart. It would tear *them* apart if he couldn't put it behind him. *"What did you do?"*

He pulled himself up and looked her straight in the eye. "What did I do?" His mouth twisted. "I killed my own brother!"

Chapter Thirteen

Shocked as she was, Annabel tried not to show it. "Simon, come and sit down." She pulled him to the sofa and held his hand as they sat down, showing him with her eyes that she knew full well the kind of man he really was, that a man so caring and humane couldn't be the monster he was making himself out to be.

"Whatever you did to your brother," she said with calm certainty, "it wouldn't have been deliberate."

The blue eyes flickered under her steady gaze. "No? My father believed otherwise, that I wanted him dead. He accused me to being insanely jealous of Robert—Bobby—and leaving our side gate open deliberately so that my brother could wander into the next-door neighbor's pool. When Bobby drowned, I thought my father was going to kill *me*. He gave me the thrashing of my life and called me a malicious, cold-blooded murderer."

Her breath caught, horror in her eyes. His own father! No wonder Simon's torment had gone so deep. "How old were you…when it happened?"

"I was seven years old. Old enough to know right from wrong. Old enough to take care of my baby brother when trusted to look after him. Bobby was just four. I loved him, but I *was* jealous of him. Everyone idolized him, spoilt him rotten, especially my father. In his eyes, Bobby could do no wrong. I don't know what evil demon prompted me to leave that gate open."

"Simon, you were only seven! Kids that age are naturally careless. They act without thinking of the consequences. You were too young to be left in charge of a four-year-old."

"You sound like my mother. She never blamed me. She blamed herself for leaving me in charge and not watching us herself. She stuck up for me and my father didn't like it. He blamed her as much as he blamed me, and treated her like dirt after that. He couldn't even bear having me around. He walked out one day and never came back. Good riddance," he growled.

"You never heard from him again?"

"Divorce papers came a few years later, from Western Australia. He wanted to get married again. That's the last we heard of him."

"So you don't know if he's alive or dead?"

"I don't know and I don't care."

She searched his cold face, his flat, hard eyes. Was that true, or *did* he care, deep down? Was his father's brutal rejection still a nagging canker inside him, tormenting him as much as his guilt over his baby brother? How would he ever get over his brother's death if his father's accusations and callous rejection were still eating into him?

"Maybe he's had time for second thoughts, for regrets," she said, expecting a stinging backlash from Simon. She waded on before it could come. "It happened nearly thirty years ago. He must wonder about the son he walked out on and treated so cruelly, wonder how you are, how you turned out."

A derisive snort showed what he thought of that. "I'm sure he has other sons to replace the only son he ever cared about. He wouldn't have given me another thought—not a charitable one—a sentiment that's reciprocated. After he left us, my mother's health went downhill. She took on all the guilt and blame herself, and she worked too hard, took on too much, got stressed out. I'm convinced that's why she ended up with a brain tumor. I blame myself for that, as well."

Her heart squeezed. All these years he'd been bottling up this terrible guilt and self-blame…not just over his brother, but his mother, too. If he couldn't let it go…

"Simon, you also blamed yourself for our daughter's death, until you finally came to accept that it wasn't your fault, that she was beyond anyone's help and you had nothing to do with it."

She paused to let that sink in, then said, "In your brother's case, you've made up a hundredfold for leaving that gate open. You were only seven, my dearest, and a seven-year-old boy can't be held responsible for an *accident*. The drowning was accidental, you couldn't have *known* what would happen, nor be held responsible for your father walking out on his family."

She took his rough tanned face in both hands and said tenderly, "*I* don't hold you responsible, my darling. I know the kind of person you are, the caring man you are. Your mother would be proud of you. And if he only knew you, your father would be, too"

The twist of his mouth told her otherwise, but in his eyes she saw relief, softness, love...for *her.* He'd told her his dark, shameful secret and she hadn't condemned him for it, or turned away in disgust. He'd been expecting her to, she was convinced of it. That was why he hadn't been able to talk about it, why he'd allowed his feelings of guilt and self-loathing to eat at him all these years.

And it would explain why he'd fallen into such black despair after Lily died. It must have felt like history repeating itself. Yet another death of a close loved one to feel responsible for.

"You've paid your penance, dearest," she said, gently stroking his unshaven cheek. "You've devoted your life to healing people, saving lives, doing for others what you couldn't do for your mother, always thinking of other people before yourself. I'm very proud of you, too. Now tell me...how is Robbie Dwyer?"

"Robbie?" His blue eyes gentled. "He's doing okay. Matt and Molly are with him. We're hopeful. He's a tough kid. A little miracle."

"He would have had no hope if you hadn't been there when he fell down that cliff."

His eyes turned bleak. "If I hadn't been able to save him, it would have been like losing my baby brother all over again. They were so alike. The same blond hair, the same cheeky grin, almost the same name...it was uncanny."

Ah, she thought, so that's why he was so affected by Matt Dwyer's snowy-haired son. He reminded him of the brother he'd...

"Maybe he came into your life for a reason," she murmured. "So you'd be there for him when he needed you."

He tilted his head and kissed the palm of her hand. "I don't deserve you."

She drew back. "You can stop talking like that, for starters. We're equals, remember. Neither one of us is any better or more worthy than the other." She slid a hand round the back of his neck. "Both of us have family influences and shadows that have shaped our lives and driven us to achieve our goals. Yours set you on the path of healing, mine on proving I could succeed in the macho corporate law world and do as well or better than the men. We deserve each other."

She pulled him closer and pressed her lips to his, and that was the last either thought of anything else but each other for quite some time.

When Simon roused himself from sleep some time later, he saw that she had her eyes open and was wide awake. He was still holding her in his arms, making it difficult for her to get out of bed without disturbing him. She'd stayed put to let him sleep.

God, he loved her. He wondered if she knew how much she meant to him. Never more than today...the ready way she'd refused to accept that he was the monster his father had made him believe he was. She believed in him, trusted him, understood him in a way he'd never dared hope or expect. The worst nightmare of his life was more like a bad dream now, almost a distant dream already. One that he could deal with.

He smiled into her lovely green eyes and pulled her closer, drinking in the scent of her hair, the sweet fragrance rising from her skin. He felt his body stir, and gently drew back.

"I'm sorry…how long have I slept? How long have *you* been awake?"

"It doesn't matter. We have all day." She snuggled back into him, and that was enough to reignite the fires in both of them. Time and the world outside became meaningless as a flood of passion and love swept them into a world of their own, a dizzying world of rapturous sensation where only the two of them existed…until his cell phone rang and forced them reluctantly apart.

They looked at each other, sudden fear in their eyes. The hospital?

Robbie?

Simon leapt out of bed and burrowed into his discarded jacket for his jangling cell phone. "Simon Pacino."

"Ah, Simon, it's Marcus Greenway. Hope I didn't wake you."

Marcus! Simon's heart dropped. It couldn't be bad news now. Not now. "What's wrong?"

"Nothing's wrong. Robbie's fine. It's you I'm calling about."

"Me?"

"Great write-up in the paper this morning. Front page. Well done."

Simon scowled. "I had no idea that woman was going to sell those damned photographs to a newspaper. She said she wanted them for her mother. It was totally un-ethical."

"But great publicity for a nonworking neurosurgeon who's just come back to Australia. I've had calls all morning from hospitals and the media wanting your phone number."

"You didn't give it to them?"

"Well, some. You might get an offer you can't resist."

"I told you, I'm going into research. I start next week."

"Well, I'm hoping I might change your mind. I have the best offer of the lot. I didn't think yesterday was the time or place, or I'd have put it to you then."

"What are you talking about?"

"I need to cut back on my hours…"

"*You* need to cut back?" He felt immediate concern. "*Why?*"

"I've some minor health problems. I'm looking for a good neurosurgeon to share my workload…and take over from me when I retire. You could start now, get your hand back in by working with me for a few sessions a week to begin with. No pressure."

"Marcus—"

"I understand your reluctance, Simon, after losing your baby daughter. A terrible tragedy. But nobody—not even you—could have saved her. I've spoken to doctors who were there."

"It's not only—"

"Don't give me an answer now. Sleep on it. You must be in need of a good sleep. I hear you sat up all night with young Robbie. That's dedication."

"He's a special case. A mate."

Greenway sighed. "You'd be wasted in research, Pacino. Give me first option, okay?" He hung up.

Annabel had thought about having a shower while Simon was on the phone, but instead stayed in bed to listen. And to watch *him*. Simon was a sight to behold with no clothes on. Riveted as she was by his phone call—his side of it, at least—her avid gaze was riveted on his well-toned physique. He looked magnificent! A bronzed Adonis with power and grace in every muscle.

But she still took in every word he said.

Her eyes flicked to his as he switched off his cell phone, meeting his quickly veiled gaze with a query in her own. She'd heard enough to know what the call was all about.

"Marcus is cutting back his hours and wants you back in neurosurgery. Right?"

Simon shrugged, and it was all she could do to keep her eyes fixed on his face and not flicking downward again, to drool over his powerful muscles and smoothly tanned skin. And more… She swallowed, her cheeks growing warm.

"He'll find someone else," Simon muttered.

"He doesn't *need* to find anyone else. Neurosurgery is where you belong, Simon, where everyone wants you to be, where you'll be happiest and do the most good. I want you to be happy, Simon. Fulfilled. Doing what you were destined to do. It's what you want, too, deep down. You're just thinking of *me*. Wanting to make *my* life easier."

"Both of our lives, I hope." His eyes were tender as he stepped back to the bed and stood looking down at her. Suddenly she was conscious of *her* blatant nudity as she lolled uncovered on the bed. Conscious of something else, too. Of her skin heating under his hot gaze.

"If you insist on staying in bed with nothing on," he murmured, "don't blame me if I come back to bed. Or are you ready to have your shower?"

"Are you?" she asked provocatively.

"If you are," he said, and his body showed her just how ready he was.

No more was said for the time being about Marcus Greenway's offer.

They were clearing up after a late lunch when Simon's cell phone rang again.

"Let's hope it's not bad news from the hospital," he said, thinking of his young mate Robbie. "Or any other hospital calling," he added in a growl. He didn't want to field off more job offers. There was no way he was going to back down, change his mind. "Simon Pacino."

"Ah, Mr. Pacino. Apologies for calling you at home. My name is Mary Buckle. I'm director of the Gumnut Hospice at St. Ives. The Children's Hospital gave me your number."

A *hospice* was chasing him now? He raised a bemused eyebrow. Terminal patients in need of a neurosurgeon? Not likely. Maybe she just wanted a donation. Or to ask him to sit on their board of management.

"Your father is a patient in our hospice," Mary Buckle said. "Tony Pacino. Antonio Pacino," she spelt out.

Simon went still. For a second, the room tilted. "You must be mistaken." He had to force his voice to work.

"My father—if he's still alive—lives in Western Australia."

"He came back from the West when his health began to fail. He went down very rapidly and was eventually brought to us. He has terminal cancer and won't live... much longer. I saw your name and photographs in the *Herald* this morning and showed them to him. I thought you might be related, Pacino being such an unusual name. He has no relatives, you see, no one to visit him or—"

"What about his wife?" Simon cut in. "His *second* wife."

"She died a couple of years ago. They had no children." Mary pressed on, undaunted. "The moment he saw your name in the newspaper, and your photographs, he said at once, 'This is my son.' He was very affected by the sight of you, and what he read about you."

Simon was unmoved. "I don't have a father," he said curtly. "He stopped being my father thirty-odd years ago."

"Dr. Pacino...Simon...your father is dying. He may not last the night. He wants to see you. He's desperate to see you. He told me he tried to find you when he first came back to Sydney, but he heard you'd gone overseas. After that, he became too ill to do anything more about it. Time is running out for him..."

"So now he's dying he wants to offer a peace pipe, is that it?" Simon made no attempt to soften the harshness in his voice, or in his face. His father had shown him no pity when he'd most needed it. He didn't deserve his son's pity now, just because he was dying.

He felt a hand on his arm and became aware of his wife's presence, sensed her sympathy. He wasn't sure if it was for him or his father. He turned back to the phone. "I'll think about it. Thank you for letting me know." He switched off before Mary could put more pressure on him.

"I know how you feel, Simon, but you must go and see him." Annabel was looking up at him, her clear green eyes glistening, showing her love for him, her understanding. "You'll never get closure if you don't. Your father and what happened in the past will haunt us forever."

He heaved in a labored breath, the argument making sense. "I'll go and see him for *our* sake…for the sake of our marriage and our future together. I won't be going because I feel anything for him. I don't. I never will."

She nodded, satisfied. "Do you want me to come with you?"

"Of course. We do things together from now on, remember? I want no more secrets between us. Whatever he has to say, and whatever I say to him, you should hear it. But you may not like it," he warned.

"Whatever happens, I'll be there for you," she said, and smiled, looking at him with absolute trust in her eyes.

The hospice was on a quiet leafy street. Trees and flowering shrubs flanked the single-story red brick building. A peaceful place to spend your last days, Annabel thought, clasping Simon's hand as they walked in. His face might have been carved from stone. He was bracing himself for a possible last cruel blast from his father. The father who'd called him a malicious, cold-blooded murderer.

But his father *had* made an attempt to find him. And now he was dying, and he must know it. Surely he wouldn't want to go to his maker with hatred and bitterness in his heart. But if he did try to reconcile with his son and extend an olive branch, would Simon believe in his father's deathbed change of heart and accept it?

His father would know now that his son had dedicated his entire life to making up for that one thoughtless act at the age of seven. He'd been shown today's glowing newspaper article with the photographs of Simon—one on the front page with the caption, HERO DOCTOR SAVES BOY'S LIFE, above the words, *Renowned neurosurgeon Simon Pacino,* and another on page five showing Robbie perched aloft Simon's shoulders, with a brief account of Simon's successful professional life devoted to saving others.

Surely his father had come to realize how bitterly harsh and unfair he'd been to his traumatized surviving son, and how deeply it must have affected him. But— she felt a tremor of unease—this was a man she didn't know and couldn't predict. A cruel, heartless man who'd coldly and deliberately abused and rejected his son, leaving him scarred for life.

She squeezed Simon's hand as they walked into the hospice together. If his father said anything—anything at all—to open up the old wounds or to hurt Simon, he would have her to deal with. Dying or not.

Simon closed off all emotion as he followed Mary Buckle into his father's room. It was a single-bed room, pleasantly furnished, and bright enough despite the dull day outside. But it lacked any flowers, family photographs or greeting cards to show that anyone loved him or cared about him.

He forced his gaze to the bed. And was shocked at what he saw. This couldn't be his father, this small shrunken figure under the covers, the sallow, sunken face, the wispy fuzz of gray hair. He remembered his father as a huge, powerful man, as strong as a tank, with thick black hair and tough, harsh features. How could he have wasted away to this extent?

"He's asleep," Mary said, "but don't worry, he sleeps most of the time. I'll wake him. He'll need to eat soon anyway." She bent over the bed. "Mr. Pacino, your son is here. Wake up, love." She raised her voice a notch. "Your son has arrived. With his wife."

She stepped back to make way for them.

Simon looked down just as his father opened his eyes. Another shock. His father's eyes, once as blue as his own, were pale and sunken into his face. They had a glassy film that made him wonder if his father could see. Until they focused on him.

"I didn't think you'd come." His voice was weak and barely audible. A stranger's frail voice.

"My wife persuaded me." Simon inclined his head, indicating Annabel.

The sunken eyes moved with painful slowness to the woman at his side. "Good woman," he murmured, a faint glimmer in his pale eyes. "Don't let her go…the way I did your mother."

Simon flinched. He was tempted to retort, *You didn't let my mother go, you walked out on her,* but he refrained. If his father regretted it, that was something. A bit late, however. Far too late.

All this was far too late.

"You weren't happy in your second marriage?" he

asked his father impassively, still feeling nothing. Mary Buckle had slipped quietly from the room, but he knew she wouldn't be far away.

His father grunted. "Married for convenience. Owned a real estate business together. Long hours. Always busy. But successful. Made lots of money."

"Good for you," Simon said, and frowned, feeling a flicker of déjà vu, reminded of his own marriage, before Annabel ran out on him. *Long hours. Always busy. Made lots of money.* He didn't relish sharing any traits with the father he despised.

"I want you to have it," his father said.

Simon recoiled. "I don't want your money." Was *this* his way of saying sorry? *If* he felt sorry. Felt anything.

"I've no one else to leave it to."

"Then leave it to a charity."

"I would have…if I hadn't found you." He tried to draw himself up. He seemed anxious to say more, but talking was obviously an effort. Annabel slipped her hand free and moved to the head of the bed, adjusting his pillows so that his head and shoulders were slightly raised.

He seemed barely to notice. His sunken eyes were fixed to Simon's face. "I see you've made something of your life. A brain surgeon! A son of mine, a brain surgeon! You must have worked hard to achieve what you have. You've done well for yourself."

"If you're about to say you're proud of me, save your breath. You don't have the right."

His father looked up at him with his pale, hollowed eyes. "You've hated me all these years?" His frail voice wavered. "You still hate me."

Simon steeled his heart. "I hated what you did to my mother. I might have deserved your abuse, but she didn't. I take full responsibility for my brother's death. I always have." He bent lower. "Why did you want me to come? You want me to hold your hand and tell you how sorry I am for what I did thirty years ago? Killing the only son you ever cared about?"

Annabel touched his arm, and he realized he was losing his cool, showing he still had feelings. He damned well didn't. Not for his father.

"I was too hard on you." For his father, it was a massive admission. "I realized it…in the end. You were only a kid. Just three years older than…"

He couldn't say Bobby's name, after all this time. He still felt it, still grieved. And yet—almost too late—he'd tried to find *him*, the son he'd despised and called a cold-blooded murderer. And he was even admitting he had regrets.

Can I believe him?

Simon realized for the first time that it didn't matter what his father thought of him, that what had happened all those years ago barely affected him any more. The old demons, the burden of guilt he'd carried for so long, were no longer eating at him, weighing him down.

"I left home because I was afraid I might harm one of you if I stayed." His father's voice was becoming fainter, harder to pick up. "I was angry. Distraught. Sick with grief."

"We suffered the same grief," Simon reminded him.

"I know." It was an obvious struggle for his father to speak, to stay focused on the conversation. "I heard your mother died of a brain tumor. Is that why you decided to become—"

"I've given up neurosurgery," Simon said flatly. He inhaled, then said roughly, "Too many people close to me have died."

His father absorbed that for a moment. "That kid in the Blue Mountains didn't die. You saved his life. And kept him alive." He held out a shaky hand. Simon had no choice but to take it. It felt shockingly frail and bony…nothing like the powerful hand of the man who'd once thrashed him to within an inch of his life. "I saw the kid's picture in the paper. He looks like my Bobby. Is that why you tried so hard to save him?"

My Bobby, not *our* Bobby, Simon noted, accepting that his father would always feel that way. *He's still mourning his favorite son. He only wanted to see me because he has no one else, and he knows he won't be here for much longer.*

"I would have tried my best to save any child," he said heavily, then added honestly, not wanting to lie to a dying man, "Well, okay, maybe the resemblance…" He shrugged, and made a further admission. "I've spent my whole life regretting what I did to my brother. And hating *you*. Yes, I *have* hated you all these years. You broke my mother's heart and spirit when you walked out on us. She'd already lost a son. You left her with nothing. She had to work her butt off to survive. I'm convinced the stress and hard work caused her brain tumor."

His father winced. "I *had* nothing—in those days. I was just starting out in real estate. I moved to the west coast to start a new life. I worked hard…to help me forget." His voice was becoming more labored, difficult to hear, but he was intent on saying what he wanted to say. "But after a time...I felt curious about you. About how you'd turned out. I wanted to see you. To tell you... sorry. I did try...after my wife died. I can see...you're a good man."

His head flopped back, his eyes fluttering closed.

"We're tiring you. We'd better go." Simon turned his head, hoping to signal to Mary Buckle. But there was no sign of her, and his father had started speaking again, every word a noticeable effort.

"You have children?"

"No," Simon said shortly.

"Pity. My second wife didn't want children," he said, his eyes still closed. "She was a career woman. No time for children."

A career woman...no time for children...

Annabel noted how still Simon had become. Was he thinking back to when *they'd* first met? *She'd* been a career woman who hadn't wanted children. Not back then. Lily had come along unexpectedly. But she'd never regretted having her baby. She only regretted not giving her beloved daughter more time and care in the short time she'd had her.

It would be different next time. Very different. If there *was* a next time.

Would Simon resist having more children because she was still a dedicated career woman? A high-flying corporate lawyer who'd now achieved a partnership? She frowned. Even if he was prepared to risk having another child, after the trauma of losing his first, would he want to take that huge step, make that commitment, with a wife still absorbed in her own career?

Maybe he *would* take the chance…if he kept working in brain research, with its regular hours and evenings and weekends off. But it would be highly unlikely if he went back to neurosurgery, with its long, demanding hours. With two deeply committed working parents…no, children would be out. What would have changed? She and Simon would barely have time for each other.

The dying man's wavery voice brought her back to earth. He was clutching Simon's hand as if he would never let it go. "You're the only one I have left. My only living relative. That binds us. I…need to know you've forgiven me."

Simon's brow shot up. "You're asking me to forgive *you*? After what I did to my brother?"

"Kids are careless. They don't think. You acted without thinking of…what might happen. I *knew* what I was doing."

Simon heaved a sigh. More a sigh of release than sorrow, Annabel thought. "There's no need for forgiveness…on either side," he said, his voice gentler now. "What happened is behind us. I'm here for you now. Is there anything you need? Anything I can do?"

What happened is behind us. I'm here for you now… Annabel could hardly believe what she was hearing. He'd put it all behind him. She could see it in his relaxed stance, his calmer profile, the way he was holding his father's hand, putting it gently back under the covers.

His father was lying back now, his eyes closed again. If he'd fallen asleep, it was a comfortable sleep. There was no sound of deep or raspy breathing. He looked very peaceful, as still as…

Mary Buckle swept back into the room just as Simon turned around with sudden concern in his eyes. "I must have worn him out. I hope he's…"

"No…you've given him peace, done him nothing but good. He was very agitated, thinking you might not come. He needed to talk to you. That was all that was keeping him going."

She bent over her patient and touched him gently, feeling for his pulse. "He's slipping away. Would you like to stay with him? In a few minutes, he'll be gone." When he nodded, resting his hand on his father's arm, she straightened. "He's at peace now," she said softly, before moving away. "And he's happy. See? There's a smile on his lips."

And, amazingly, there was.

Chapter Fourteen

Annabel wanted to stay at home the next day to be there for Simon and to help him arrange a private funeral for his father, insisting that Guy would understand and give her another day's grace. But he insisted she go to work.

"If you don't sign those partnership documents they might retract their offer," he said, a tender light turning the blue of his eyes even bluer.

"Well, I would like to finalize things," she admitted, and smiled happily. She had reason to feel happy. Simon finally had the monkey off his back. He'd thrown off his demons, reconciled with his father before it was too late, and the difference in him was enough to give any wife a warm glow. The future looked good.

"Good for you," he said, and kissed her. "I'd also like to go to the hospital to see Robbie."

"Yes, of course." She wondered if he would speak to Marcus while he was there, to discuss the neurosurgeon's tempting offer. But that would be too much to hope for. Simon would need more time for that…and maybe a little push, she thought, in the right direction. Her heart fluttered at the thought of what she was planning to do.

"And you have all those calls to answer," she reminded him, getting back to immediate matters. His mobile phone had a string of unanswered messages stacked up, waiting to be dealt with. Mostly from hospitals, but also a few from the media, seeking interviews. She knew he wouldn't be returning *those* calls.

"I'll get round to the most important ones eventually," he said, shrugging. "The media can go jump."

"Well, I must go and get ready. Call me a cab, would you, to be here in half an hour? You take the car."

"We're going to need a second car. If I have time, I'll start looking around. I don't start work until next Monday."

We'll see about that, she thought, a dreamy light in her eye as she skipped off to get dressed.

As Simon put candles on the dining table, to go with the silverware and wine glasses, he sniffed appreciatively, proud of the spicy aromas rising from the kitchen. He hoped his dinner would taste as good as it smelled. And that she wouldn't be too tired to enjoy it.

It was already growing dark and rain had started to fall outside. There was even thunder and lightning about. A real winter's night. But they'd be snug inside the apartment, sipping champagne to celebrate her partnership. He found himself hoping the new demands on her wouldn't change their lives too much, take her too much away from him.

It would be up to him to make sure that didn't happen.

The moment he heard her taxi pull up outside, he lit the candles and rushed out with an umbrella.

She gave a chuckle when she saw him. "Well, this is service," she said, as they scuttled back inside.

"Thank you, ma'am. So you think I'd make a good valet?"

"I think you make a better neurosurgeon," she returned lightly, reaching up to kiss him on the lips.

"You don't give up, do you?" he drawled when he was able to speak.

She didn't pursue it. She'd noticed the lighted candles on the table and the silver and glassware, and was sniffing the piquant aromas drifting from the kitchen. "Simon, you've cooked dinner!"

"Don't sound so surprised. I can cook, you know. I just never had enough time before."

Her smile wavered. "Neither did I. But I intend to change that. I'll just throw off my coat and change into something more comfortable." She danced off before he could ask her what she meant by, *I intend to change that.* Was she determined to help with the cooking on the nights she was able to get home early? Was that what she meant?

When she came back she was in a slinky pale green leisure suit of some shiny stuff, with pink velvet slip-ons on her feet. Her hair, which she'd worn short in Venice, had grown quite a bit since then and was already curling round her neck, almost to her shoulders, making his fingers itch to run through it, the way he used to when it was flowing down her back. He wondered if she was growing it again for him.

"You look good enough to eat yourself," he said, thinking ahead to the moment he would do just that... taste her all over.

"I didn't think baggy sweats would go with your romantic candles and silverware," she murmured, and opened her eyes wider when she saw he'd poured two glasses of champagne. "What's the celebration? Is Robbie out of danger?" He saw her eyes light up. "Or is this a special wake for your father?" she asked gently, and smiled serenely, confident she could mention his father's name to him now.

He gave a bemused shake of his head. Typical of her to think the celebration was for someone else, not for her. "Robbie *is* out of danger, thank God," he said, "but it's not him I was thinking of, you duffer, or my father, though I'd be prepared to drink to him, too, something I never thought I'd want to do. No, it's *you* this celebration is all about, my beautiful, deserving wife. Are you all signed, sealed and delivered? Can we now officially drink to the esteemed new partner at Mallaby's?"

She pursed her lips, her eyelashes sweeping across her eyes. "Let's drink to Robbie first, and then your father. And *then* we'll talk about me."

"I'm prepared to do that," he conceded, understanding that she'd want to take time giving him all the details of her partnership. "To young Robbie," he said, touching his glass to hers. "An intrepid, amazing, extremely lucky young man, if ever there was one."

"To Robbie," she echoed warmly. "Our miracle boy. The miracle only possible because of his unbelievably brilliant, caring doctor...and best mate."

Their eyes met as they raised their glasses and sipped, each thinking of what might have been if Robbie hadn't survived his fall, or if medical help hadn't been at hand. They even spared a thought for Lorelei, whose photographs and unwanted publicity had done some good after all, bringing Simon and his father back together.

"And here's to your father," she said softly, "who found you in the end and made his peace with you before it was too late."

"To my father...and what might have been," Simon said, and they sipped solemnly. "And now," he said, refilling their glasses. "This one's to you, my darling. To your—"

"Wait," she said. "Let's just drink to *us* first...to our future...and then I'll tell you all."

"Okay. To us...and our glowing future," he said at once, the burning tenderness in his eyes telling her all she needed to know, nothing held back.

"To us," she echoed, and they sipped again.

Annabel knew the time had finally come. Why was it so difficult to tell him? She gazed up at him, loving him more than she ever had before, knowing more about him than she thought she would ever know. But she still didn't know how he would feel about the one thing that had begun to matter most to her.

She dragged in a rallying breath, and said, "I've decided not to take up the partnership offer—unless they agree to a part-time arrangement, which they're considering. I'd like to start a family…if you feel ready, too"

She felt his shock, and waited, holding her breath. She wasn't sure if it was the first part or the second that shocked him more.

This time he took a large gulp of champagne, not just a sip, before he spoke. "You *can* have both, you know. A full-time partnership *and* a family. We'll do it differently this time. We're older and wiser and won't be so driven, so obsessed with clawing our way to the top. We've learned from our past mistakes. We'll make time to live a little, enjoy life. And I'll have more time to help out."

"You're saying…you'd be happy to have another baby?" She could hardly believe it. That he could be so accepting, so quickly. "You're not just saying it because I——"

"I'm not. I'd be very happy to have another child. With you." He lifted his hand to rest it on her cheek, his warmth seeping into her, balm to her soul. "I'm ready if you are. Lily will always be a part of us…" for a brief second pain flickered in his eyes, and she knew he would see it reflected in her own…"but we can make room for other children, too"

Children? Was he thinking of *more* than one eventually? She reached up to cover his hand with her own. "I'm glad you feel that way," she whispered, a husky whisper. "And I love you even more now, if that's possible."

She looked up at him with a determined glint in her eyes. "I want to do it properly this time, give any children we have all the time and care they deserve. *Need.*

And I couldn't do that as a full-time partner at Mallaby's, with its added pressures and responsibilities."

"But a partnership's what you've worked so hard for, what you've always wanted, aimed for."

"It *was* my goal, yes, and I've achieved it, something my father never believed I could do. I've proved something to myself…and to him…that I can reach the top and be accepted as an equal with the men. But my priorities have changed. I've told Guy I'll be leaving Mallaby's when I have the baby, unless they let me take a year or two off to be with the baby, and then come back on a part-time basis. They're going to let me know."

"You'd be prepared to leave *Mallaby's?*" Simon gripped her shoulders. "Are you serious? You'd give up your *job?* But you love your job. It's meant everything to you, from the moment I first met you."

She looked at him in dismay. "You think it meant everything to me? More than you? More than Lily? Oh God, if that were true…but it's *not,* my darling. I just let my damned ambition rule my life. I let my father's warped attitude rule my life, too It made me lose sight of what really matters. You…us…our children…*life.* I don't want that to happen again. I don't care any more what my father thinks or might say about it. I intend to work part-time or not at all—at least for the first few years of our babies' lives."

He searched her face. "There's no need to risk your partnership. We can share the child care, share the workload. You can't throw away all your legal knowledge and experience. Besides, you'd miss the mental and intellectual stimulation."

"I'll still get that working part-time. If Mallaby's won't agree to it, there are plenty of other part-time jobs for lawyers with my skills and experience. I've heard about a women's legal service that would really interest me and benefit other women, women who badly need legal help. And I could pick my own hours."

She reached up to kiss him. "You don't mind me giving up full-time work, do you? I promise you, this is what I want. To be a wife and mother, first and foremost, and to be there for our children…and for you…until they're ready for school, at least. But can we afford it?" she asked, looking up at him with wide eyes.

"Well, I won't be earning a fortune doing research, but no worries, we'll manage."

"Of course we will." She drew in a quick breath. "Whatever you end up doing. Research…neurosurgery…if you decide you want to go back," she added hastily. "Working part-time, I'll have more time for *you,* my darling, a chance to make *your* life easier. Why should all the giving and supporting come from you?"

She looked up at him, searching his eyes, gazing deep into the swirling blue. "Follow your heart, Simon. If surgery is where your heart lies…'

"It isn't," he said softly, placing a gentle hand on her breast. "This is where my heart lies…with yours."

Her eyes misted, her heart beating faster under his touch. "That's a lovely thing to say, darling, but I—I meant your *working* heart," she corrected, not wanting to let this chance slip. "Surgery is where you'll be happiest, my love, where you're most needed and will do the most good." She was convinced of it. She'd seen the yearning in his eyes, seen the signs, in his capable, caring actions, that his thinking was changing. "Marcus must agree, or he wouldn't be chasing after you. He's giving you a chance that most surgeons would jump at."

"You know what it did to us before." He lifted his hand to drag his long surgeon's fingers through his hair. "The long grueling hours, the time we spent away from each other, the stress of making life-and-death choices…"

She put a tender finger to his lips, knowing he was thinking of Lily when he spoke of life-and-death choices. "People understand that no one, not even the greatest surgeon in the world, can heal everybody…but *you,* my dearest, can give them their best chance. And you won't *need* to work the long hours you did before or take on so many cases. You *wanted* to work those killing hours before. You *had* to. You were still proving yourself, honing your skills, making a name for yourself. You wanted to be the best and you *became* the best." *And after our daughter died, you worked even longer and harder, to try to forget, to blot out the blackness in your heart. That's all behind us now.*

She looked up at him, her eyes appealing to him to let her finish. "Now that people recognize you for the great neurosurgeon you are, you can choose your own hours, only take on the cases that fit into the schedule *you* want to keep. Please, darling," she begged him, "think of yourself for once, and what you really want, what'll be best for you…for both of us," she was quick to add. "If you do decide to go back to neurosurgery, a lot of very sick people will reap the benefit, and I know you'll be happier than—than doing anything else." Gulping in a breath, she finished in a rush. "And you'll earn more money and I won't feel so guilty about cutting back *my* long hours."

He looked at her doubtfully, a glint of suspicion in his eyes. "If you're sacrificing your own career because of *me*—"

"No!' she denied sharply. "Oh Simon, haven't I convinced you yet? I want a family…children…and I want to be there for them. And for you." She sniffed in the aromas from the kitchen. *Time for a diversion.* "You're not letting our dinner spoil, are you? It smells so delicious, and I'm starving."

"Hell, I need to stir something!" He released her and leapt for the kitchen.

Simon's chili con carne was a big hit with his wife. He had to smile at her squeaks of delight at each mouthful, and the way she had to douse the hot chili with numerous glasses of water.

"Simon, this is simply delicious…you ought to be a chef! How will I ever be able to compete with a meal like this?"

"We're not in competition," he reminded her, enjoying the bright emerald sparkle in her eyes, knowing it was more from the hot chili than the quality of his meal. "We're an equal partnership, remember…it's give and take…doing what we can for each other, when we can. If I go back to neurosurgery…" He saw her eyes light up even more at this first indication that it was a possibility "…I won't be working at the same pace I did before…or taking on so much. I won't take on the job of chief neurosurgeon when Marcus retires but I might consider working *with* him, or with whoever takes his place. I want to enjoy my marriage, and have time to spend with you…and any children that come along."

My God, he thought, *children.* For so long, he'd never dared contemplate having more children, never believed she would *want* another child, let alone ever consider giving up the partnership she'd worked so hard for just when she was on the brink of her greatest triumph.

He delved deep into her eyes, trying to read the truth behind the sparkle. She'd assured him that this was what she truly wanted, that she wasn't giving up her full-time career for *him,* simply to ease his way back into neurosurgery, and maybe he should believe her, that it was her marriage and family she was thinking about, first and foremost.

Whatever the real truth was, he could see she was genuinely happy about her decision.

Tomorrow, he thought, I'll go and see Marcus. It won't hurt to talk about his offer, at least. And I'll look into those other offers…

He pushed back his chair. "Ready for dessert?" he asked her. "I've marinated some fresh strawberries in Grand Marnier and whipped up some King Island cream."

"Mmm, it sounds yummy." She pushed back her chair, sidled round the table in her slinky gown and tugged at his hand. "But it will keep until later, won't it?" Her voice was low and wickedly seductive, her lovely green eyes gleaming with promise. The promise of earthy, rapturous delights right now, and more lasting, even more satisfying delights stretching into the future. A happy, fulfilled future together, with another child—or *children*—to bless them even more.

"It can keep marinating forever as far as I'm concerned. I'm in your hands. Now and forever."

"Oh, Simon, I do love you. So much."

"Ditto," he said, echoing what she'd said once. "I can't tell you how much."

She smiled, perfectly happy with that. With everything. "You don't need to tell me. Just show me."

"My pleasure. Now…and for the rest of our lives."

* * * * *

If you enjoyed what you just read,
then we've got an offer you can't resist!

Take 2 bestselling love stories FREE!

Plus get a FREE surprise gift!